AS THE PIZZA BURNS

DEDICATED TO:
Andrea, Josh, and T.C.

You were taken from us much too early, and your shadow continues to guide us into the forever that you've become. Your short presence on this earth was a blessing and the footprint that you left behind is larger than the world will ever realize. Thank you for blessing me with your existence and friendship. It's in my proudest moments that I can hold my head high and tell the world that I knew you. I am and always will be in your debt.

Act 1

CHAPTER 1

According to Pizza Corp corporate office, POS stands for Point of Sale—but *we knew what it really meant.* Hooked up to a white keyboard and mouse from the mid 1990's, the order-taking interface woke from its sleep in much the same way a ninety year old man would—if he had gone to bed with a liter of Nyquil and ten shots of vodka. I jerked the mouse for a few moments and after the screen finally lit up, I answered the phone.

Corporate policy is to answer each call before the third ring. *Hilarious.*

I zoned out into the abyss of the computer screen, thinking about how my request to have that day off had been approved months ago, but there I was. My wife Trinity, the woman six months pregnant with my child, was holding her birthday get-together that day and I was stuck working... Such is life, I suppose.

All things considered, I wasn't surprised that I had to come in. Even on my days off I'd somehow find myself there for eight hours. At that point in time, I hadn't had a single day off in over two weeks. The worst part was I still only got paid for five days at a time. Even if I wasn't in uniform, I found myself washing dishes or tossing chicken wings. At least, that's what I was *expected* to do. If I thought the store was burning down on a normal day, I would have hated to see what would happen if I wasn't there.

At the very least, I was able to make a quick run to get Trinity a present before I made it in... and I just barely arrived in time.

The present was worth the trip, though. The design was flawless—it matched the tattoo Trinity had on her left wrist. It was in the shape of two rings intertwined.

This is what it looked like:

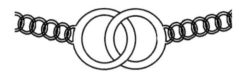

I had no idea when I'd have the time to give it to her, but I'd been eyeing that thing for weeks. I guess that sums up our situation—some husbands give their wives cars, clothes, and all kinds of other expensive shit for their birthdays... but me? I hardly had the money to give her an aftermarket necklace.

"Thank you for calling Pizza Corp, this is Tony," I said. "Will this be for delivery or carryout?"

I hurried to put my code into the terminal and arrived at the main screen, which gave me those two options—delivery and carryout. These are the only two buttons and the terminal requires one of them to be pressed before any order can be taken.

Hey, don't look at me. I didn't design the thing.

I waited rather impatiently for an answer, flicking my finger against the terminal keyboard, but the man at the other end of the line muttered a loud grunt and remained indecisive for a good forty-five seconds. This was normal.

"Yeah," he said after a long, heavy groan. "I'd like some chicken wings."

"Will this be for delivery or carryout?" I asked again.

"Oh," he said, "what's the difference?"

What's the difference?

"One's where you drive," I said, "and one's where we drive."

"Yeah," he said, "that one."

That one.

"I'm sorry, sir," I said. "Which one?"

"Uh…" he said, "delivery."

"Delivery," I said. "Excellent."

I clicked the delivery option on the terminal screen, which promptly asked for the customer's information, starting with their telephone number. This, like the last screen, must be completed before the customer actually orders anything.

"May I have your phone number, please?" I asked.

"Yeah," he said, "give me an order of boneless wings."

"Definitely, but may I have your phone number, please?" I asked.

"Buffalo."

During my off-shifts, there was another shift manager that no one really liked to work with. In case anyone reads this, I won't say her actual name. Instead, let's just call her… *Crabby.*

4

This is what Crabby looked like:

Several months prior, the previous store manager was let go and Pizza Corp didn't have a back-up. So, in the heat of the moment, they gave *all* the administrative privileges to *Crabby*, who was clearly the most qualified out of the two of us. *#dashofsalt.*

She'd hoped that corporate would at the very least send her to development training or give her some sort of promotional opportunities, but sadly, toward the end of it, they admitted to her that there weren't any plans to advance her. Of course, they also didn't bother increasing her pay, which made her that much more... well, *crabby* about the whole shebang.

So, in that last few weeks, not only was she more flustered than ever, she had started to ignore her normal tasks and essentially let the store drag along. Schedules were sloppily made, truck orders were missed and the store ran out of supplies nearly every day. Thus, the employee morale was at an all-time low—*even for Pizza Corp*—which, needless to say, was a sad, *sad* panda. Luckily, this madness was about to stop. The next morning, we'd actually meet our new store manager. I was excited, but I kept my expectations low. It was Pizza Corp, after all.

Now, every night when the PM manager clocks in, Pizza Corp's policy states that the opening manager is required to give him or her a "tour" of what the store looks like and help him or her develop a "plan of action" about how to get it in shape before it closes.

With Crabby, this typically went one of two ways:

A) I'd walk in, she'd grunt at me, throw me the clipboard, and then promptly march out without saying a word. In the brief period of time after she left and before the orders started to come in, I'd take a quick peek to find that the store's a total train wreck, come up with an action plan myself, get with my workers for the shift, and then *as a team* we'd start our *inevitably shitty day.*

B) I'd walk in and she'd have a *huge smile* on her face. *It was weird.* She'd walk me around the store and brag about how busy it had been and how she was able to make the store so immaculate… and then she'd leave. When that happened, I'd go to the one place that she

6

hadn't gloated about and discover the three thousand dirty dishes that were crudely stashed there. After assigning that *ungodly task* to someone who *clearly didn't deserve it,* I would then come up with an action plan myself. I'd get with my workers for the shift and *then* we'd start our *inevitably shitty day.*

Unfortunately, yes. No matter what happened, the outcome was always the same. Eventually, we *had* to start our *inevitably shitty day.* Every day.

Fortunately, that day, Crabby had tossed the paperwork at me and left.

After that few long minutes, I went back to surveying our situation and quickly found out that Burt, one of my workers for the night, was scratched off the list without anyone added to replace him.

Sounds like Crabby's handiwork.

I was sure there was a note hidden somewhere that said,

"Burt's on vacation," or more likely, "Burt works at Sonic on Sundays but I scheduled him anyway, like an *ass-basket*."

Quotes may not be exact.

Worst part was, on the last page of the clipboard in big, bold letters, there was a note telling me to "SAV ALL THE LABER U CAN."

Crabby.

Naturally, I did the opposite. I went to the back and attempted to call someone to come in.

At the very back of the store, there was a metal desk which, if it weren't for the help of the dishwasher and the shelves on either side, would have fallen apart years ago. It held an old computer that must have weighed eighty pounds and had a Windows 98 sticker but was instead given Windows XP. Yes, for those reading this, Windows XP had stopped being supported a long, long time ago. This day and age, we have watches with more power than that "office computer."

Ever since I first started working at Pizza Corp, there had been a Batman mini-action figure which sat in various places on that desk… and *every once in a while* someone would move it around so the next person who sat there would have a momentary burst of heartfelt wonder about how and when he moved. It was… *amusing.* This, however, only lasted until someone put a toy rope around his neck and hung him from the

Pizza Corp 'District Customer Experience Winner, 2001' trophy with a note that read, "You either die a hero..."

Batman hadn't moved a single time since then.

I kissed my fingers and placed them on Batman's head. It was something of a tradition. Then I pulled the schedule up, which of course took a few minutes, and eventually got to the view where I could see the entire week. I immediately found out that Crabby had taken Burt completely off today's schedule, which meant that if I added anyone it would screw the entire labor system up for the week.

The labor system is a piece of software incorporated into our scheduling system that budgets the amount of work hours we're allowed to schedule. It usually uses the speed in which an "average worker" can perform certain tasks and measures that against how busy the day is forecasted to be in terms of sales dollars. Not only is Pizza Corp's labor system wildly off when it comes to predicting sales and measuring performance, it also spirals completely out of control when the schedule is tampered with—especially after numerous times.

Oh well, zero shits.

I searched for someone who was off that night and, preferably, most of the week. That way, we wouldn't have to worry about going over twenty-five hours. Pizza Corp is obsessed with part-time employees staying under twenty-five hour workweeks and usually takes strong disciplinary measures against the part-time worker, the manager on duty, and the store manager if an employee breaks that rule. They do this because if an employee averages out to at least thirty work hours per week, the government considers them to be "full-time" and requires Pizza Corp to offer them healthcare benefits. This is a *problem* because Pizza Corp does everything humanly possible to *avoid* giving employees health care benefits.

Anyway, I found Max. She was only scheduled to work fourteen hours that week and was off that night. Plus, she'd been asking for more hours as it was. Max was my first pick anyway. I pulled out my cell phone and gave it a shot.

"Hey. What's up?" she asked.

"Hey Max. One of the people working tonight can't come in. I was wondering if you could help close," I said.

"What time do you need me?" she asked.

"What time can you be here?" I said.

"Hold on a second."

She put the phone down and took a few moments while I started editing the schedule. I pulled everything up and set the cursor on Max's name, awaiting her arrival time. I waited for a few minutes while she figured things out. She was a single mom so I understood how crazy it could get just to have a minor change in plans. After a while, she got back on the phone.

"Hey, you there?" she said.

"Yep," I said, "what's up?"

"I think I can get there by seven…" she said and thought about it for a second. "…Yeah. I'll leave Dominic with my Mom at six-thirty and drive over there. I'll be there at seven."

"Awesome," I said, "thanks!"

"It's no problem," she said. "But one more thing."

"What's up?" I asked.

"Well…" she said, "you're going to be there tonight, so I guess I'll just ask you then."

I typed her into the schedule and got off the phone. She was probably going to ask about the new schedule, since she had put in her availability request nearly a year earlier and it hadn't been approved. Crabby, *being Crabby*, typically rushed through making the schedule and didn't give the slightest thought to approving any sort of employee request. The manager before Crabby had taken a similar attitude—it was the nature of the beast. I usually tried to help Max switch shifts with other workers so the kind of shit that happened today with Burt didn't happen with her.

I heard that familiar ringing sound from the front of the store, which meant someone had put that freaking "Ring for Service" bell back up front. The ring itself admittedly wasn't terribly annoying, but when the customer rang it several times because we didn't just pop out of thin air, it became a problem. Really, all we used it for was bugging each other. The only time it was *actually out* was when corporate was paying us a visit.

I made my way up to the register, greeted him, and clicked the carryout button on the screen.

"How are you?" I asked, to which he gave no response.

He removed his sunglasses and peered toward the menu for a few minutes. I clicked impatiently with the mouse as I waited for him to finally decide to order a Large Pepperoni—because that's what everyone orders when they have no fucking clue what they want. I typed the order into the screen, waited for a few minutes and was just about to go back to work when he finally decided to say something.

"Yep," he said, "I think I'll order a pie."

Oh, good. Chocolate or apple?

"What size?" I asked, and waited to see if I had to change anything on the screen.

"Um..." he said, "Large."

"What would you like on it?" I asked.

He thought about it for a moment, looking at menu as though he was about to win the million but was out of life lines and unsure about the answer.

"Pepperoni?" he said, taking a leap of faith.

"Excellent," I said and looked toward the back. "It will be

ready in about in fifteen minut—"

"—No, wait," he said and thought about it for a moment.

"Sausage." he said, nodding at the menu and giving it a menacing glare as if it had cleverly fooled him into buying something that he'd never want. That menu was *such the businessman.*

I waited for a moment, giving him time to change his mind. He said nothing, but was still hurriedly reading the menu. I hovered the mouse pointer over the button to remove the Pepperonis and waited for him.

"... Um, no," he said, "never mind. I'll have pepperoni."

"Excellent," I said and completed the order, "It will be ready in about fifteen minutes."

I thanked him and went back to survey what I had left to do before the rush.

The order-screen lit up and made a sound more like a squeal than a beep. Juan slammed a tray on the make-table and looked at his phone.

"Hey Tony, Crabby didn't have a cook and called me in this morning," said Juan. "I'll make this pizza, but after that I have to go."

I looked back at the schedule, which still had Juan as my cook.

Fuck.

I couldn't keep changing the schedule... the labor for the week would absolutely *shit itself.* I was hoping that Max would replace Burt as our CSR, but it looked like she'd have to cook. That's what I got for coming in early to help Crabby and not taking the extra step to make sure *my shift* was covered. Before I could fully process it, the make-table screen lit up and beeped again. Then it did it again... and a third time.

"Later!" said Juan and let the door slam behind him.

I took a quick peek at the screen by the fryer, on the other side of the kitchen, to make sure no one had ordered wings, and I darted to the make-table and put some gloves on.

Reece, a driver, took a mad sprint to the delivery screen— and after the first two orders came out of the oven, he sliced the pizzas himself and went on his way.

Since we didn't have another driver coming in until seven, he knew he'd have to take all of them... and as I started the first pizza, the phone rang once again.

I hated Sundays.

I heard the door-chime, which meant a customer was walking in. I thought for a moment about if there were any carryout orders that I had taken. I couldn't recall any, but I realized that there were six or seven internet orders that I hadn't started yet. To put it lightly, I wasn't prepared for another customer, let alone another customer inside the store. Pausing for a moment, I stepped away from the make-table and went to check to see if I needed to greet anyone at the counter, but no one was there. I darted toward the pizzas forming a blockade at the end of the oven. Some of them were halfway burned, some of them were burned halfway, and half of them were just burned. It was only by coincidence I managed to catch a glimpse of a familiar butterfly backpack.

Max to the rescue.

It took her a minute, but I heard a few things move around in the back of the store by the office PC. It was her usual routine, at least when she worked with me. A few months after she started, she figured out that she could disconnect the audio cables from Pizza Corp's broken speaker system and hook them up to her boom-box, then connect the boom-box through Bluetooth to her phone. With that convoluted series of connections, she could play whatever music she wanted over the restaurant's speakers. Originally, Pizza Corp designed those plugs to broadcast its own "hand selected" music throughout the kitchen, but the disk-player broke and was never fixed.

It's not exactly Pizza Corp Process but it's what kept Max happy. And a *happy Max* makes *happy pizzas*. It's not like customers could hear it over the sound of the oven anyway.

Suddenly, the speakers jolted with the sound of percussion. She popped out from behind me and just started working. She didn't need direction. I'm sure she saw me making pizzas and just knew what kind of night we were having. She hopped past me, opened the cooler to my right, looked at the screen and just started going to town. Pushing me out of the way, she opened the cooler on my left and got another pan. Then another.

I tried to stay out of the way and I went to the cut-table, where there was just a big stack of boxed pizzas with no hint about where they were going. One by one, I put them in bags, put the ticket inside, and sorted them by priority and location so Reece could just grab and go.

Looking back at the make-table, Max was definitely making a dent. She was pumping out pizzas like bullets from an M-16. That still didn't solve the driver problem, though. In the back of my mind, I remembered that a few more employees were supposedly going to show up around that time. Keeping Crabby in mind, though, I had to entertain the idea that I would have to make a few more changes.

I logged into the drivers' computer and checked to see how many new customers we had on the list—and it was full of them.

At Pizza Corp, or virtually any delivery chain, drivers are required to call all first-time customers back to confirm the order before they take a delivery—someone could rob or kidnap a driver.

What sucks is Pizza Corp's online system catalogues customers by their email address, while the in-store system logs customers under their phone number—meaning, due to slight mismatches, pretty much every customer is considered a new customer. We couldn't call *all of them.*

So... what did we do? We clicked the button that *says* we called them.

And that's exactly what I did.

"Hey," Max shouted, "while you're up there, what's the address of number one-sixty-one?"

"365 Emerald Circle." I shouted, "Apartment 267."

"Awesome," she said.

"Why?" I asked.

"I forgot the beef on one of their pizzas," said Max. "That place never tips though, so it's okay."

"Oh." I said. The small managerial voice in my head made me think for half a second about telling her to remake it, but common sense got the better of me.

While I was there anyway, I checked that order off of the callback screen, as well as all the other new customers.

"Good." I said, "I guess."

I heard the driver door slam open—from around the corner,

Mike peeked his head in. He acted as though he was afraid of walking in, but I knew better. He was there to work. He wanted us to ask him to come in. He always had a flair for the dramatic.

"Hey, Mike," I said.

I debated for a moment, deciding whether or not I wanted to play his little game. Ultimately, I knew I'd have to if I wanted him to take some deliveries. That night though, I really didn't have the time.

"Oh," he said, "hey there, Tony."

"What are you up to tonight?" I asked, knowing the answer.

He took a deep breath and made a long, dramatic, sigh. Walking past the corner, he made an entrance that he considered to be critically flawless. As if the fate of the store relied solely on his taking a few boneless wings out of the fryer.

The alarm started to go off. I started to run toward it but was forced to concentrate once again on the blockade of pizzas outside of the oven.

"Oh," Mike said, "you know..."

Oh, I knew alright.

"You want to clock in?" I asked.

"Well," he said, "you know me..."

Distracted, I pulled an incorrectly sorted pizza out of the bag and placed it in its proper stack. Things were quickly starting to get convoluted. I didn't know the time, but I was sure it was after seven o'clock. The other drivers weren't coming. I *needed* him to clock in. It couldn't wait any longer.

"You've never let me down before," I told him.

"Hmm..." he said and looked at his watch.

He was such a drama queen.

"*Yeah...*" he said, "*I guess...*"

"Can you get those wings and take some deliveries?" I asked.

The bell rang, and in what seemed like a blink of an eye, an elderly lady made it up to the counter. My hands were tied. I had pizzas going every which way, and some were still getting lodged at the end of the oven. I couldn't go up front. Looking back toward the make-table, Max was making progress but still wasn't there yet.

"Is one of you going to help me?" shouted the lady.

Without an answer, Mike headed toward register number two and clocked in. I continued to process the orders at make-table, and before long I saw him finish punching in her order and run back to the fryer.

A few moments passed by before he put some orders of chicken in delivery bags and headed out on his first delivery. The chicken wings, like the pizzas, were burned to a crisp. It wasn't long before the calls started flooding in. It's not a Sunday if no one complains.

A few hours had passed and the night was almost over. Mike stayed a while. After the deliveries died down, he finished most of the dishes and left shortly afterwards. He was never fond of staying after close. The orders still came in, but they were much slower and gave Max some time to clean the make-table while I cleaned the rest of the store.

The lobby was a wreck. During the rush, there were a few families of ten to fifteen that ordered a bunch of pizzas at the same time and ate them in the lobby. It took Max and me combined about half an hour to make each of their orders. Needless to say, they weren't thrilled. They left us a giant mess. One of them wrote out "Thanks for the quick service" in marinara on one of the tables.

The phone rang once again, and Max stopped what she was doing to answer it.

Reece still had two more deliveries to take, so he was going to be out for potentially the rest of the evening. Maybe the person on the other end of the line would understand that we were about to close and decide to order somewhere else.

"Thanks for calling Pizza Corp, this is Max, will this be for delivery or carryout?" she said. "Um, yeah. We close at eleven o'clock. You've got about... seven minutes."

"Awesome!" said the customer. "Just in time!"

Figures.

Max took the order while I finished up the lobby. I started cleaning the fryer and washing the rest of the dishes while she made it. During the next thirty minutes or so, it was pretty quiet. Reece picked up the last orders and took all three of them—of course we had to re-clean the mess we'd made when we'd prepared the last-minute orders, but overall it went alright. Max and I just spent the time closing up. Since the new store manager was coming in the morning, the store had to look perfect. Not only did I want to make a good first impression, but you never knew when Mitch or Lindsay from corporate would stop by. I didn't think they would, since it would be first thing on a Monday morning, but I didn't want to chance it.

After everything was clean and all we had left to do was mop the floor, Max pulled me aside.

"Hey, Tony. Can I bother you for a second?" she asked.

"No problem," I told her, "what's up?"

She turned around and noticed a splatter on the shelf and vigorously wiped it off. She was stalling. It didn't bother me. Whatever was going on, I knew I'd be happy to help. It was tough though, and I think Max knew that. Switching shifts on weekends or evenings was impossible... but for Max, I had to try.

"Max," I said, "talk to me. What's up?"

She sighed.

"I know you've helped me out a lot... and I really appreciate it," she said. "I was just wondering if you could change something for next week."

"What's that?" I asked.

"Well," she said, "you know how the doctors are saying that I need to hurry about scheduling Dominic's major surgery?"

I nodded.

"I'm... well, I'm still not ready for that," she said. "He didn't exactly react well to any of the smaller surgeries... and every time I ask, they remind me about the risks associated with this one."

Her hands jittered. She bit her lip. Her eyes tightened as she attempted hold back her tears. She was always good at holding back her tears, which bothered me. No one should *have* to be that good at it... and yet for some people, it's their greatest skill.

"So," I said, "how can I help?"

"I've scheduled one more small surgery," she said. "I plan on taking the leap and scheduling the major surgery next month."

"Alright," I said, "just let me know."

She nodded.

"I'm scheduled to open on Wednesday next week. That's the only time they're available for the surgery," she said. "Do you think you can help me switch it?"

I smiled at her, at least, to the best of my ability. I wanted to assure her that everything was going to be okay. Coming from me, I knew it didn't mean much. But I hoped at least another smiling face would help.

"I bet I can," I said. "Don't worry. I've got you."

It only took us a few minutes to sweep and mop. Max asked if she could make one last pizza to bring to her son. I couldn't say no. I made one for Trinity and myself as well. By the time that was finished, Reece made his way inside. I cashed him out, finished all of the cash duties and closing paper work, and finally locked up. Another Sunday was over. As we walked out, Reece quickly drove away and I was left with Max once again. She pulled her phone from her pocket and sighed.

"My ride's running late," she said.

Pizza Corp wasn't exactly in the best area. I wasn't about to leave her there in the dark. Pulling out a pack of cigarettes, I sat on the curb and watched the guys over at Sonic take out the trash.

The smoke filled my mouth with that warm, filling taste that it always did. I often found it surprising how comfortable the Pizza Corp building could be when I was standing outside of it. Max put her purse and pizza boxes on the ground and took the cigarette I offered her.

For a while, both of us just sat there and waited. We'd engage in unspoken conversation by making impressed faces about the odd shapes that our exhaled smoke would make and we'd groan casually at muscle cars and loud motorcyclists that drove by. For the longest time, though, we didn't say a single thing.

"I've never been much of a smoker," I said.

She peered toward my open box of cigarettes as I reached for my second or third one and chuckled.

"I quit about a year ago," I said. "You know what they say about peer pressure. This is *clearly* your fault."

"Oh, *whatever*," she laughed.

It was true though, I hadn't smoked in nearly a year. Obviously, Max didn't get me back into the habit, though. It was a very stressful time for me and I found myself spending a lot of my free time just sitting at places waiting for things. Not just at Pizza Corp; sometimes at the Medicare office, the mechanic, waiting for my wife to get off from work, everywhere. After a while, I just went to the gas station and got some. It felt more natural than I thought it would. I figured I'd at least feel guilty, but other than feeling poor I didn't feel much of anything at all.

Max's eyes rolled. She looked toward the butt of her cigarette and played with it between her fingers for a few moments. Eventually, she tossed it out and looked back toward the ground, making a long sigh.

"Well, yeah. I hadn't smoked for a while either," she said.

"What does *that* say about peer pressure?"

I honestly had no answer—I just wanted to make conversation so she wouldn't feel as bad about her ride showing up late. It was actually nice to have any sort of excuse to have interaction with someone, even if it wound up being awkward and quiet.

"I don't smoke around Dominic," she said, "So that's at least something, right?"

She took another cigarette and lit it. Then she sat for a while, looking at the pavement and playing with the cigarette with her fingers. She looked like she wanted to say something but couldn't figure out how to word it. She did that a few times, actually. She'd open her mouth, sigh, and kick one of the concrete rocks into the small layer of grass between parking lots. Eventually, though, she ran out of rocks.

"Look," she said, "I know this sounds… kind of weird, but I just wanted to thank you."

"For what?" I asked.

She looked around in a brief panic and found some more rocks from behind her. She kicked one of them so hard that it flew over the grass and into the parking lot of the Sonic next to us.

"Just for, you know," she said, "working with me and my son. I know I've requested a lot of time off for his surgeries and

I'm sure you think that I'm just being an overprotective parent. Everyone does."

I scooted closer to her, grabbed one of her rocks, and threw it. I couldn't see where it went but I was satisfied just to know that it wasn't there anymore. I liked the way she scurried to find something to do when she got nervous. It was amusing.

"I don't think that," I said, "and if anyone does, I haven't seen it."

"You didn't see Crabby's face when I told her that I made the appointment," she said. "And like I told you, she scheduled me anyway."

Crabby—I just didn't understand her. She was self-centered, constantly angry... and she never seemed to have a reason behind it. If it came to a choice between working just a little harder at Pizza Corp or taking care of herself, Crabby always chose the latter.

"Yeah, well Crabby doesn't have kids," I said. "Most people who haven't had kids don't understand how hard it actually is. Especially if he has a medical issue."

She grabbed another rock and threw it the same way I did. I didn't see where this one went either.

"Well, that's just the thing," she said. "If it was just Crabby that would be one thing. But it's everyone. People who work here, people who don't... *everyone.* I see other parents at the grocery store just staring at me because I can't let Dominic bend over the seat in the shopping cart."

"Well, he has spinal problems," I said.

"Yeah, but they don't know that. All of their kids are healthy, so to them it's absurd that I'm so strict with his movement. They just look at me like I'm an idiot while all of their kids are throwing stuff and making a big mess," she said.

I sighed. I hate them. They're all the same, everywhere they go. Everything they do. They're always so... judgmental. They're rude, disgusting, hateful, and needy. Worst of all, they're fucking *everywhere.*

"Anyway, I just wanted to thank you," she said. "Thank you for making the situation I'm in livable."

"It's my job," I said.

"No. It's really not," she said. "That's the reason I've stayed down here so long. Not everyone tries as hard as you do to make people happy."

I sighed.

"What happened?" I said. "I mean, you know, before you moved."

Up to this point, I'd worked with Max for nearly a couple of years, and I never had time to actually talk to her about her personal life. I knew a little, sure. I knew that she was trying to divorce her husband. I knew that she had moved down here from

Delaware. I knew that she lived with her son in an apartment—
that was it. But every time I had the chance to find out something
new about her, I took it. I can't explain it. Maybe it was that she
was so misunderstood by everyone around her. Maybe it was that
she always worked so hard and made so little. Maybe I just
couldn't fathom how she was able to do it all. I don't know.
Whatever it was, it was interesting. *She* was interesting.

"Well, Patrick and I got married when I was sixteen and he
was eighteen," she said. "When we moved up there, we had no
one. I was hours away from anyone I knew. He had to work two
jobs and I had, you know, to work... but we were making it."

She threw another rock, and turned around to look for
some more. After a few moments, she gave up. Leaning back on
the wall, she gathered her thoughts.

"We weren't, you know, doing great or anything," she said,
"But we were making it."

"And then?" I asked.

"Well, a few years later, we found out that I was pregnant,"
she said. "All I'll say about it is... he wasn't... thrilled."

"What do you mean?" I asked.

She tilted her head down and puffed her cigarette a bit
more, watching the smoke as she exhaled once again.

"It's okay," I said. "If you don't want to talk about it, we
don't have to."

She made a long sigh and picked up another rock. After examining it for a good ten seconds, she threw it like an out-of-practice baseball player. It rocketed toward the sky and after a few moments we heard it crash onto Sonic's roof. She thought about it and sighed again.

The Sonic guys were becoming rather unamused about the whole ordeal. I waved passively to one of them. He returned the wave and threw back one of the rocks. It's funny… sometimes, that's all it takes.

"Well," she said, "at Dominic's first birthday party, Patrick asked me if we could give him up for adoption."

"Seriously?" I asked.

"Yeah, seriously." she said.

I picked up another rock, but I knew that I couldn't throw it as far as she did. Well, maybe I could. If I tried, though, I'd probably end up failing all over the place. So, I stretched my arm back to make the appearance but ended up gently tossing it into the grass. It got her to chuckle. She got another rock and handed it to me. So, this time I actually tried to throw it. Reaching my arm back, I rocketed it into the air as high as I could. After a few moments, it plopped into Sonic's parking lot.

"It's just a weird concept," she said, "to have your relationship with your husband going smoothly, but for him not to get along with your son.

29

"He told me a few times that he didn't even love Dominic. He said he doesn't... really think of him as a part of our family."

She held back a few more tears and I wasn't exactly prepared for it. I could tell she'd been through a lot, but I wasn't expecting what I heard. And I had a feeling that this was only beginning to scratch the surface of what she was doing there, leaning on Pizza Corp's brick wall. If there's one thing I've learned while working at Pizza Corp, it's that no one works there because they *want* to.

We went back to watching the smoke from our cigarettes, after that. It was just easier. I could tell that Max had probably had enough with telling me about her life anyway. I felt guilty for even asking.

"Gah," said Max, looking at her phone.

I chuckled at her. "It's okay."

"No, it's not. I can't believe I told my mom that I had a ride," she said. "'No mom, that's okay. I don't *need* the car. I'll have a *friend* pick me up.'"

She started getting a little flustered. I didn't exactly know what to say, so we spent the rest of the time kicking rocks and finishing our smokes. About fifteen more minutes passed by before a piece of trash mini-sedan drove into the parking lot. It drove all the way around... slowly... and when it pulled up, the guy inside nervously opened the door and moved a bunch of garbage and college textbooks out of the way so she could sit down.

We gave each other a quick wave and they drove off. I took a small moment to finish my cigarette and enjoyed its heat against the cool October night.

Watching the car drive away, I let the ten million midnight thoughts figure themselves out...

I wished that I could have talked to her a little longer. I definitely wasn't into Max *that way*, but in a lot of ways I thought she was interesting...

I don't know.

Maybe I just felt lonely with everything I had going on in *my life*. Maybe I just wanted to keep talking to... *someone. Anyone.* My wife was definitely asleep at home... and I hadn't seen a *friend* in years. I doubted I even had their phone numbers anymore.

I looked up to the Pizza Corp street sign, which in my view was the only thing luminating in the night sky, and pushed the thoughts back as much as I could.

But the truth was... *I was alone.*

After a brief minute, I made peace with myself. I went home, jumped in bed and got up bright and early to meet our new store manager.

CHAPTER 2

I walked in. It was eight o'clock in the morning. I didn't *have* to be there. No one specifically *asked* me to be there, but I wanted to meet our new store manager... even if it meant spending a few more unpaid hours at Pizza Corp... and let's face it, that was nothing new anyway.

I heard the bittersweet sound of mariachi, which meant Juan was the opening cook. No wonder he was in such a rush to leave the day before. As I walked around the corner, I noticed that all of the lights were off except for the ones he was using. Meaning Crabby still wasn't there. Before saying anything that I might have regretted, I poked my head about the store just to make sure. Yep, lobby lights were off, back of house PC lights were off, and the restroom lights were off. It was starting out to be quite the peaceful morning.

"How's it going, Juan?" I asked.

He reached toward his phone and paused the music. While he stretched the hand-tossed dough, he turned his head around to talk.

"Hey, Tony," he said.

Physically, Juan was intimidating as all get out. With essentially the body of a retired professional wrestler, his tattoos stretched across the entirety of his skin and said something offensive in just about every language. His hair was buzzed, his beard was grown, and he wore a hairnet instead of the standard Pizza Corp hat for no other reason than to bring attention to the bull's-eye that was tattooed on his forehead.

After getting to know him, most people realized how hilariously harmless he was. He not only preached the "Core of the Corp" (a terrible saying that corporate continued to blat out, hoping to inspire teamwork), but any time he heard anyone curse or say something the tiniest bit demeaning, he'd preach the power of Our Lord Jesus Christ. The weirdest thing, though, was when he'd do it, people would listen. I could never tell if it was because they were genuinely interested in what he had to say or they were so shocked that it was coming from someone who looked like him. Either way, it was pretty neat.

"Is Crabby here?" I asked, knowing the answer.

"Nope," he said, "you know she never shows up until after nine."

I went back and locked the door, then I walked over to the PC, sat down, and started booting it up. It took a few minutes, but I treasured it and passed the time by sipping my coffee and holding it tightly against my cheek, letting the warmth soak into my skin. We were halfway through October so it wasn't like it was terribly cold, but it was cold enough to enjoy the coffee's heat. After the computer booted up, I started printing everything that Crabby would need for her opening paperwork. If I was going to be there, I might as well make myself useful. I started stacking it together when I heard a knock at the back door.

I walked around to make sure I wasn't hearing things, but no one was there. Then, I heard the knock again. It was definitely coming from the back door. Weird. Crabby definitely had the keys, and I didn't expect her for at least half an hour. You'd think that corporate would give our new manager a key. The knocking continued, so I went ahead and opened it.

It was George, a driver. He was dressed in uniform, so he

was obviously there to work, but why was he there so early?—oh, wait. Juan needed someone to be inside the building with him. That was probably Crabby's excuse. So that's where all of our labor had been going. The more I thought about it, the more I thought about how it was going to suck for the borrowed manager that night. Juan and George were our only two Spanish speaking employees and Crabby took both of them. However, the thing that surprised me the most about this whole ordeal was how much it surprised me.

"Hey, George," I said.

George flattened his eyebrows and stepped back. Squinting his eyes and curving his lips outward, he locked his arms straight. In one swift motion, he pulled a bag from his pocket as if he were in a Japanese Anime and then, like a robot, launched his hand toward my face, halting it inches away. The sands of time dragged along as George swung the bag in front of my eyes.

You'd think with all of the importance he put into the bag, he would've been handing out drugs.

"BossMan," said George, "I've got gummy worms."

This is what a gummy worm looks like:

Gummy worms are fruity candies that are, go figure, shaped like worms. They're usually covered with some sweet or sour coating and are loved by kids of all ages. Especially George, as it turned out.

I didn't reply. George had the tendency to talk. A lot. In fact, in my entire time knowing him, I can only recall three times that he's been speechless. I didn't mind, he was a funny guy, but before I said anything that could potentially start this avalanche I needed to go back and figure out if he was actually scheduled for that morning. I knew Crabby was a lazy ass, but I refused to believe she'd stoop to that level. I hurried back to the office machine, pulled the schedule up and printed it. Scrolling down the schedule, I found him. Luca Martinez. There he was. Eight o'clock.

Yes, Luca is his real name. George is a nickname. It's wise not get him started on it. He'll never stop.

Walking back into the kitchen, I noticed that George had already hopped on make-table to help Juan with his prep. I was going to ask George if this was turning into a regular thing, but by the way George was expertly stretching the dough and perfectly distributing the sauce, it seemed pretty obvious. After a few moments, George jammed his hand into the bag and pulled some gummy worms out, laying them carefully on the make-table between them, sharing some with Juan.

"You know, Tony," said Juan, "if the new manager sees you guys in here, he's probably going be really mad."

I thought about telling him that if the new manager saw him eating gummy worms while preparing food he'd probably be really mad. That's an enormous food safety hazard... but this is Pizza Corp. These two have done plenty worse.

"I don't blame him," I said. "If I walked in someplace and saw George there, I'd be pretty mad too."

"Yeah, right, whatever Boss," George said.

He pulled out a few more gummy worms and once again put them on the make table.

"You're not the only one," said Juan. "George, tell him about Reece."

"What about Reece?" I asked.

"It doesn't matter," he said.

"Really?" I asked.

George sighed and thought about how he was going to phrase it.

"Alright," he said, "So, a few days ago, Reece and I were right over there, bagging some chicken wings, right?"

I opened my mouth to speak.

"Right," he said, "well, he was being all anti-social. He wasn't saying a single thing. He *never* does. *He's so insensitive.* So I'm all like, asking him about his personal life. You know, trying to get him to open up, and he's not having any of it."

"Maybe he didn't want to talk to you," said Juan. "I don't usually want to talk to you."

"No one ever wants to talk to you," I said.

George lifted his cheese and sauce covered hands toward us. His face flattened. His bushy unibrow fell perfectly in line.

"Yeah. But you guys do it anyway. Reece doesn't," he said. "Anyway, after a few minutes, he started singing this One Direction song. At first, I was like, 'Oh. That's why he's not talking. He's got a song stuck in his head!' But then I started listening to the lyrics. Something about someone stealing his girl."

George's eyebrows shot to the air so quickly I doubted that his thick forehead could stop them. His arms flailed wildly and uncontrollably in front of him.

"It didn't make any sense!" said George, "I was like…

'Aren't you gay?' And he was all like, 'Yeah man!' And then I was like, 'You can't be gay and have a girlfriend! That just doesn't math!'"

George counted on his fingers as if attempting to actually solve the puzzle.

"This just in," said George, "I did the math. One plus one equals two, not 'I'm gay and have a girlfriend.'"

He took a moment to try and calm down. Gently and slowly, he started taking long, deep breaths. He bowed his head and grabbed another gummy worm.

"You can't just say something like that," said George, barely making out the words as he chewed, "You can't. It will do irreparable damage to our problem-solving skills."

I stared at him for a moment.

"George, that was the dumbest thing I've ever heard," I said. "And Juan, I'm ashamed of you for allowing me to listen to it."

"You can shut the hell up," George said and looked toward me. "Why are you here, anyway?"

"I'm waiting for the new manager," I told him.

"Oh," said George, "I'd come back later if I were you. The new manager won't be here until around ten."

I sighed.

"Really?" I said, "I just got here. What am I supposed to do, just leave for two hours and come back?"

"Well yeah," George said. "What else are you going to do?"

Well, long story short, I left for two hours and came back. I couldn't just go home and see my wife though. It would have been nice, but we were living with her parents. It was about an hour drive away. By the time I got there, I'd have to turn around and come back.

It wasn't always that way, though. We used to live much closer... and on our own. Before the pregnancy, things were happier... and much, much easier.

I was working nine-to-five in an accounting office as an administrative assistant. Trinity was working as a receptionist at a packaging company. Back in those days, I thought my life at Pizza Corp was long behind me... I hadn't worked for them in years.

A few months into the pregnancy, though, we started seeing developmental problems with the baby—after seeing about a billion specialists and emptying our *entire income* in medical bills, we finally had an answer.

Cervical cancer.

Yeah. *Fuck us, right?*

At first, the doctors said stuff like, "Oh yeah, don't worry. It's only trace amounts of *fucking cancer.* We can treat this *after* you have the baby. At most, all you'll just need an in-and-out surgery."

But then, it started getting to be more and more of a big deal. She had visits to the specialist once a week, which moved to twice a week, and before we knew it she was bed-bound for the rest of her pregnancy. I tried my best to balance everything for myself. I went to as many of her appointments as my job would let me, which consumed every last bit of my paid time off, then when Trinity had to leave the packaging company I went back to Pizza Corp as a second job to work in the evenings. I never got to see her except while we were at the doctor's office or brief periods when I had time to go home before Pizza Corp. It bothered me, sure, but I had confidence that we'd get through it.

That was, of course, until I got my termination notice from the firm.

Apparently, working eighty hours a week and caring for your wife *who has cancer* can cause your performance to drop. Go figure.

I tried to apply for other jobs. Believe me, I tried. I even set goals for myself. I had daily application counts and told myself that if I got a job with pay over a certain amount that I could quit Pizza Corp—*for good this time.* I spent hours upon hours every night just staying up applying for jobs, using every website imaginable. I lost countless hours of sleep... but it never happened.

I was stuck at Pizza Corp.

Things started to look bleak. We started getting behind on rent. Our power got shut off once a month for three months in a row. My credit union threatened to repossess my car. It was ugly. So, what do you do when you have a low paying job, a wife with cervical cancer, debt higher than your nose, and pink slips flooding out of your ears?

You move out. Back in with your parents—well, back in with *her* parents.

So, after careful consideration, it was settled. We moved in with her parents and I stayed with Pizza Corp. Like I said, no one works at Pizza Corp because they *want* to. Everyone has their reasons.

It was tough waiting until ten. I wished that I could have just gone home, but I wanted to take action. I wanted the new manager to know that not only was I a hard worker, but I was also dedicated. Not only was Pizza Corp my family's only lifeboat, but it was the only thing I had.

I drove around for a few hours... just listening to music and staring into the abyss of the road ahead of me. Passing the time, I thought about what life might be like after the baby came. After we'd figured out how to get Trinity better. After we'd *somehow* gotten ourselves back on our feet. After all of this went away. The problem was… I didn't know how we'd get to that point. I knew that I had to get promoted so I could make more money to support the baby, and I knew that Trinity would have to have the baby to start fighting the cancer, but that was all I knew. I didn't know how I could *afford* to take care of a baby or get Trinity her treatment for *cancer.* I didn't even know if I was going to have enough gas in the tank to make it to work every day.

I felt like I was sitting on the sidelines. Other than earning just enough money to keep us from going under, I didn't know how to help.

Trinity was sick… she was really sick. A few nights prior, I'd received a text mid-shift telling me that she was in the hospital. I tried to call everyone from my store and neighboring stores to get someone to relieve me but I wasn't able to leave until after the store closed. It was almost midnight when I finally met up with her at the hospital. Her whole family was there, as was some of mine.

Earlier that day, she had gone from specialist to specialist, checking in and out of office after office. Just being moved along, with little to no information. She didn't know what was going on with the baby or herself. When she left the third office, she started to notice a trend. All of the doctors did the same tests, they studied the same facts about previous tests, and they told her the same jargon that the other offices told her. After a while, the offices started to close and they moved her to a local emergency room, where a doctor finally stopped and took some time to catch her up on the whole thing.

Inside of the womb, there was something called a "potentially malignant mass," which is another way of saying, "something that we don't know what it is." It could have been cancerous, it might not have been. They didn't know. Either way, it wasn't there before and they had no way of going in and checking. The slightest disturbance could hurt the baby. After I finally got there, they moved everyone out of the room but Trinity and me. They sat us down and told us, up front that was going to be hard for Trinity to have this baby. Not only hard, but dangerous. Even with a C-section, if the baby moved the wrong way or if the mass started to grow, she could hemorrhage and we could lose both of them. Worst of all, there wasn't anything they could do about it. There wasn't any surgery they could perform. We were six months pregnant... there were no treatments available for a case like this. There wasn't even a way of figuring out what it was. It all came down to two things: luck and money. We had neither.

After they *shat that pile of bricks* on us, they left us alone for about an hour so we could talk about the situation with some privacy. We spent the first thirty minutes just sitting there, staring into each other's eyes. I didn't know what to tell her. I didn't know how I could make this better. We knew that we had to confront the idea that she might not make it through the birth of our baby, but we couldn't get ourselves to talk about it... or even admit that it was a possibility. Instead, we just tried to get the whole thought out of our minds. Eventually she took a long sigh and asked me to bring her purse to her.

She pulled out a small pocket-sized journal and opened it up. She was making a list. So far she only had a few things on it, but she said that she'd started to write down as many things as she could. Her long-term goal was to reach two hundred.

It was a list of the best feelings in the world.

She said that there were rules that each item on the list had to have. Firstly, it couldn't have anything to do with money. Secondly, it had to come by surprise, at least on some level. Thirdly, it had to be something that could be shared with someone else.

She wanted to find a way to keep her eyes on what was good about life, so she'd always feel like she had lived her life to the fullest, even if it were cut short. We spent the next half hour trying to add as much as we could to the list.

AS THE PIZZA BURNS

At the end of the night, this is what it looked like:

The Best Feelings in the World
1. Sitting on the porch, watching a thunderstorm
2. The smell of a brand-new book.
3. Bowling a strike, especially if it's in the last round and it puts you in the lead.
4. Laughing so hard you cry.
5. Staying up until the sun rises.
6. Waking up to the smell of fresh coffee.
7. Hot Cocoa on Christmas Day
8. Falling asleep to the sound of rain.
9. Waking up to the sunlight shining in from the window. On your honeymoon. Next to the person you married.
10. Bacon. I don't care if it makes sense, it's bacon.
11. Looking outside and seeing your whole neighborhood covered in snow.

Eventually we had to let our family in so we could tell them what happened... and then we headed home. Then, just the next morning, we received the medical bills from the hospital and specialist visits.

Just from that one day, *just for finding out she had cancer*, we were sixty-thousand dollars in the hole. Three times my yearly salary. And that was *after* our insurance paid them. We spent hours on the phone and eventually worked out a ten-year payment plan, which ended up being more per month than my car payment.

But we spent the next few days looking for more to add to the list. It made a great distraction. Every time we found one, we'd text it to each other.

Eventually, the time came to drive back to Pizza Corp. I had a lot riding on my shoulders... I needed to make good impression. I gathered my thoughts, took a deep breath, and marched in.

As I strode inside, I immediately noticed the strangest thing... Pizza Corp was *quiet.*

The make table was pulled out, leaving no walking room. Juan was behind it, scrubbing away at the wall, every so often dipping the rag into a bucket of monochrome water. He looked up at me in the same way a puppy would look at his mother for the very last time and just held his eyes to mine. I looked toward the wall, which already started to show a marvelous difference between before and after.

"Looking good," I told him.

He peered back toward the wall and threw the rag into the bucket. He continued to bounce his eyes back and forth but eventually accepted the task at hand. After making a long sigh, he begrudgingly went back to work. This time, slightly more determined to actually finish it.

"Yeah, I know..." he admitted.

I turned past him and walked over to the fryer, where George also had a *special* project. George struggled as he tugged at the bottom drawer which contained a filter. That filter's job was to hold all of the grime from every piece of chicken, potato, and apple pie left over after we took them out. Corporate policy states that we change that filter *at least* once per day. *Supposedly,* it should happen in the morning. Without a store manager, however, that left the humble responsibility to Crabby. Needless to say, that filter hadn't been replaced in over six months.

With a great deal of force, George wedged it open and started sliding it out. He accidentally took a small whiff and his face went wry. Tightlipped, he examined the musky, copper-colored goo that reached far beyond the filter, burying all of the nobs and levers that George would soon have to use.

He leaned back and collected his thoughts for a moment, then gave the filter a quiet, somber nod as if to say, "*Yep... just as I suspected... it's a giant pile of shit.*"

I carefully stepped over him, avoiding any potential contact with the fryer and that dreaded filter. Walking toward the back, I could hear Crabby talking to someone but what I heard wasn't the deep, strong, corporate blabbering voice I thought it'd be. It was actually... feminine. Sure, it held the strength that you'd expect from someone of a higher authority, but it also had something I never suspected... compassion. She sounded... reasonable. *Odd.* I started to walk forward, but was stopped by a whisper from behind me.

"Tony!" George said, "BossMan!"

"What?" I whispered back.

George's face flattened. With a deadpan delivery, he let out a long sigh and continued the conversation.

"The new boss lady," whispered George, "she took away the gummy worms."

The make-table's screen buzzed and Juan made the loudest sigh of relief I'd ever heard. He washed his hands and walked past George and me, humming a familiar worship song as he strolled by. Turning the opposite way of the managers, he made his way around the loop to arrive on the other side of the make-table. George gazed up toward me, silently asking for permission to check and see if it was another delivery.

I nodded and made my way over to the back of house PC, where I found Crabby and finally saw our new manager with my own eyes.

"Hey, Crabby," I said.

Crabby acknowledged my greeting with a nod, but gave no other response. I reached my hand out to the manager sitting at

50

the desk to introduce myself.

"Hi," I said, "nice to meet you. I'm Tony."

"Oh, hello," she said, "I've heard a lot about you!"

I looked toward Crabby. If I didn't know any better, I'd say she growled back. She looked toward me for a split-second and flashed back toward the schedule. Her aura dissuaded me from making any other action toward her. There was fire in her eyes.

"I promise you," I said and looked toward Crabby once more, "It's not *all* true."

"You say that," she said, "*I'm hoping it is*. I've been hearing a lot of good things."

She shook my hand and focused back toward the computer screen. There was something she wasn't telling me. I didn't want to believe anything remotely positive, but her tone hinted that corporate might have said something to her. Which meant corporate noticed me on some level. I shrugged the thought off and pressed on. That would never happen. At least not at *this* location.

"I'm Janice," she said. "I'm excited to be here."

The weird thing was… she looked like she meant it.

Janice continued to talk with Crabby, so I started to take my leave. I wasn't exactly supposed to be there anyway, so it wasn't like I was missing anything. I stepped over George once more and walked toward the front of the store. On my way up, my foot got caught in a roller-wheel of the trashcan by the counter. My other foot slipped on the freshly waxed floor and down I went. On my way down, I grabbed the trash can for support, but it hardly helped. I ended up taking it with me. I caught myself with my elbows and the garbage splattered all over the ground. Juan peeked his head over the make-table and George made a quick hand motion toward me when they heard the noise.

"You okay, man?" asked Juan.

I tried to rub out the pain. I was fine, but my arm hurt like a bitch. I nodded and tried to get up when I noticed something inside of the pile of garbage... A broken picture frame. It was from ages ago. We used to keep in on the desk, but I guess it got thrown out with all of the cleaning that Juan and George were doing.

It was a picture of some old friends, Liz and Jeff, while they were on their wedding reception. Before the picture was taken, Jeff had worked at Pizza Corp with me for a long, *long* time. He was actually the shift supervisor that trained me. Liz was a customer. Twice a week, every week, she'd come by on the same days, at the same time just to see him. She'd order, tell Jeff some raunchy and *terribly unfunny* joke, grab her pizza, and leave. But over the course of a few months, they started *actually talking*. Then they started *dating*. A year or so went by and he proposed to her. She said yes.

After rigorous searching, he found another job, *a real job*, and put in his notice at Pizza Corp. He invited all of us to the wedding, but I think Crabby was the only one who actually made it. We had arranged to borrow a manager from another store to cover my shift, but he never came in. I got stuck working, since there wasn't anyone else who could cover it.

I scooped the trash back in the canister and looked at the photo again. They had their reception at Pizza Corp. It was the best day I'd ever worked. After that, though, I never saw him again.

I looked at the picture … Jeff and Liz were in the center, then Crabby, Juan, Max, and I stood around them. Scattered throughout were people who no longer worked with us… people I hadn't seen in ages. The team was so different back then.

I guess that's the thing about working in the service industry. People leave. No one gives it a second thought, but the last time anyone sees someone is on their last day of work. There's no goodbye, there's never a hug or any final words. Nothing. It's just another day at work. Even with the people you care about, after they clock out for the last time, they're gone. No one notices that anything's changed until there's a small reminder: a specific order, a left-behind name badge, a broken picture frame. Until then, though, it's just work... and work goes on with or without them.

However, once in a blue moon, there's someone who seems to take a piece of you with them.

I tossed the picture back in the dumpster and heard that familiar ding from the service bell. It rang again, then again. I didn't even have time to turn around before it sped up so fast it started to ring continuously.

"Anyone home?" she asked in an endearing voice.

It was Max. *What the hell, Max.*

I turned around and walked toward the counter. Dominic had the bell and was playing with it. I smiled at her for a second and typed my numbers into the screen. They didn't work. The POS froze up for a moment and brought up an error message saying that I needed to be clocked in. *That was new.*

"May I have the bell, please?" I asked.

"Can Uncle Tony have the bell?" Max repeated.

D'aww... Uncle Tony! That was new, too.

He handed it over and responded with an adorable burst of complete gibberish, followed by the only comprehensible words I could hear: "Button" and "Mommy." I think I might have heard the words "Bubble" and "Lasagna" in there, but that might have just been my trying too hard to listen.

"You know our new manager's here, right?" I asked her.

"Oh. *Shit.* Sorry," she said. "Do you think we bothered him?"

I looked toward the back.

"I don't think so..." I said, "*she's* back there with Crabby."

"She?" she asked.

Before I could say anything to respond, Juan popped his head above the make-table.

"Psst!"

"Hey!" he whispered, *"Max!"*

"Yes sir," she said.

"Shh!" said Juan. *"Be quiet!"*

She put Dominic down on the ground and let him walk around. Flailing and squealing, he was anything *but* quiet. Juan's eyes widened. He quickly jerked back behind the make-table and started cleaning again just in case Janice happened to walk by. Max took off her backpack, put it on the ground, and opened it.

"You want *Darth Vader?*" she asked.

Dominic paused. The surplus of sound echoed throughout the lobby until it was quiet enough to hear a pen drop. Dominic slowly stepped over to her and reached his arms out widely.

"Da... dar-*Darth Vader?*" he said more intelligibly than some adults do.

She reached out from her bag and pulled out an action

figure. After placing it firmly in his hand, she stood up and looked back toward me.

"That should keep him occupied for a while," she said.

"He likes Star Wars?" I asked.

She nodded.

"Just like his mother," she said.

Juan cautiously peeked over the make-table once more and peeked around to make sure Janice or Crabby hadn't come back around.

"*Max!*" he whispered again, "*You should order a pizza!*"

"Yes, Juan," she said, "that's why I'm *here*. On my *day off*. At *Pizza Corp*."

"*Shh!*"

Max squinted her eyes and made a motion with her fists, acting like she was winding one of them up like a jack-in-the-box—*suddenly* her middle finger shot up toward him. She acted surprised. Juan did not.

"George!" I said just loudly enough to get Juan's attention, "You're going to have to take her order. My numbers aren't working since I'm off the clock... apparently."

George didn't hesitate. Dumping his filthy gloves in the garbage, he raced toward the POS to take her order. I didn't stick around, though. It looked like they had it under control.

I was headed out, anyway. Before Max finished her order, I

got in my car, buckled my seat belt, and moseyed along back home.

On my way, Trinity sent me a text saying that she was having terrible cravings for movie theater nachos. Why specifically from the theater, I have no idea. It was expensive, but I couldn't tell her no. I stopped by a theater on my way home and bought some, and what the hell—some popcorn, too.

Did you know that even if you only want to buy the food, you still have to buy a ticket? Well, it's true. Whatever, though. It made Trinity happy. Plus, I chose to think about it as a small donation to the movie I liked the most.

Congratulations, Star Wars, you are now the happy owner of another twelve dollars and fifty seven cents.

Eventually I made it home to the quiet two bedroom house that Trinity grew up in. Her parents were out, so it was just us.

"How was the new manager?" she asked.

"I don't know," I said. "I didn't have a lot of time to talk to her."

I sat on the couch next to her, gave her the nachos, and put my arm around her. I didn't even bother taking my shoes off. Soon, I thought, I'd get that phone call and I'd find myself right back at Pizza Corp.

"Her?" she asked.

"Yeah," I said, "it surprised me too."

A few more seconds of silence went by while we just sat there, enjoying each other's company. I looked into her tired green eyes and thought about what life would be like after this whole thing was over. Every so often, I felt a phantom vibration from my pocket and pulled the phone out to check the empty screen.

"Maybe you'll get to stay with us," Trinity said.

She grabbed my hand and moved it to her belly.

"We both love every second we get with you," she said as I felt the baby kick and move around.

After about an hour of sitting around, being afraid to commit ourselves to anything, Trinity wanted to watch the Notebook.

Well, *three hours* later, I started to realize that maybe, just maybe, Janice had some sort of competence and could take care of things on her own.

Another hour flew by and I *started* to relax. Trinity wanted to watch a movie and wasn't too picky. I took a chance and popped in Batman Begins. The baby kicked the entire time. Baby loves Batman, just like his or her daddy.

I would've bet anyone anything that Janice was going to call me in during that movie. It was one of my favorite movies of all time. There was no way the universe would allow me to enjoy it.

But there we were—cuddling on the couch with empty food

bins as the closing credits rolled.

We put in The Dark Knight, and then The Dark Knight Rises.

After a while, Trinity fell asleep in my lap. I surrendered to taking my shoes off, but it wasn't worth changing out of my uniform. I could wash it in the morning anyway, and I still wasn't convinced that I'd get to stay home with her.

Eventually, I realized that I'd forgotten to fix Max's shift for Wednesday like I promised her I would. I needed to fix that by the end of the next day, somehow.

I also couldn't get what Janice had said out of my head. She'd heard good things... *whatever that meant.* It made me wonder... suppose she did hear something good about me. What did she have planned for Crabby? Maybe she was just being polite, I figured. Yeah. She was just being respectful.

But seriously. I must have done something right.

Right?

The rest of the night passed by. I stayed awake through most of it, just feeling Trinity's warmth against mine. As I zoned out into the quiet nothingness, I kept my hand on Trinity's belly and felt the baby move around and kick at my fingertips.

I let the weary musings of my inner thoughts take over. I hoped that maybe, just maybe I'd get to spend the rest of my life with her... after I figured out what I was going to *do* with my life. I pictured us getting up on a Monday morning, getting ready for the old nine-to-five grind. Locking the door of our three bedroom house, and putting the kids—*plural*—in the car.

Then, maybe years later, Trinity and I would grow old together and forget the nightmare that was our lives before whatever miracle happened to save us.

For a few short hours, I thought that soon the worst would be behind us... and we'd start a new life. As new people. People who were important... people who contributed more to the world than *just trying to survive it.*

I smiled at Trinity through the fog of my illogical, untamed, and endless dreams. I kissed her on the forehead and slowly, my eyes closed as I drifted away into dreamland.

It was fine, I thought. We'd be fine.

Throughout the rest of the night, I managed to start believing it. I fell asleep the most calm and optimistic person I'd ever been... and maybe ever would be.

But then... tomorrow happened.

CHAPTER 3

"Thanks for calling Pizza Corp, this is Reece. Will this be delivery or carryout?"

The phones were ringing off the hook, make-table was a disaster, the cut-table was so filthy you could hardly see it, dishes were overflowing so much they were falling out of the dishwasher, and the delivery screen was completely full.

Yep. Just another day at Pizza Corp.

"Well, yeah," said Reece, "*I guess* we're still offering that

Wednesday special. But… today's Tuesday, so that doesn't—

It was going to be one of those days.

"…But—but. Well, okay," Reece said. "Will this be delivery or carryout? *One's where you drive and one's where we drive. Yeah, which one?"*

The driver door slammed open. Turning my head around, all I could see was the black blur of a delivery bag being vigorously thrown over the top of the rack. The bag plopped down on one of the shelves and George sprinted to the driver screen and checked back in from his delivery.

"You okay, man?" I asked.

He looked at me and gave a quick sigh. Making his way over to me, he put his hand on my shoulder.

"I don't get it, BossMan," he said. "*I just don't get it.* How can someone get a delivery that costs *thirteen dollars and fifty-three cents,* pay with *fifteen dollars* and claim that he's tipping *five dollars?*"

Yes. This happens.

During football season, Pizza Corp has a special deal that offers large pizzas with any number of toppings for *"Just ten dollars!"* When you add the two dollars and fifty cent delivery charge and tax, it totals the order to the amount of *thirteen dollars and fifty-three cents.*

In fact, during football season, it's a common ritual to sing our unofficial theme song during the rush on game nights. This theme song was written by Reece and it's a constant project to get enough of us together to actually record it and eventually send it to corporate's advertising department—for them to promptly ignore. Everyone at Pizza Corp, including Crabby, gathers around to sing this song.

The chorus goes like this:

It's thirteen,

Thirteen fifty-three,

After taxes and delivery,

That two-fifty doesn't go to me,

But hey,

That's the price that you paid,

It's thirteen fifty-three,

No, it's not much to look at. But it's ours. We sing it during every football game. It's part of our shitty Pizza Corp culture I guess. If there is such a thing.

"Also BossMan," he said. "I wrote you a Teamwork Tomato."

This what a Teamwork Tomato looks like:

Teamwork Tomatoes are little cards that are used for recognition at Pizza Corp. Essentially, they're supposed to be filled out and personalized any time an employee does something that *really* they should have been doing anyway.

At the end of the month, all of the cards go into a bucket and one is randomly selected by the store manager. The employee who wins becomes Team Member of the Month and wins *twenty whole dollars.*

During corporate visits, Mitch and Lindsay would swear by Teamwork Tomatoes and told us that if our P.U.R.E. culture was strong enough, employees would start to write them to each other—however, they failed to realize that it doesn't make any sense for employees to do that. All that does is decrease their chance of winning the twenty dollars.

Our store had shit-tons of Teamwork Tomatoes, though. They were all written by George.

George didn't write them to be P.U.R.E. or to promote the "growth" of that employee or any of that other shit, though. He wrote them because he thought they were hilarious.

"Thanks," I said.

"No worries BossMan," he said, pulling it from his pocket and handed it to me. "You deserve it."

This is what my Teamwork Tomato from George looked like:

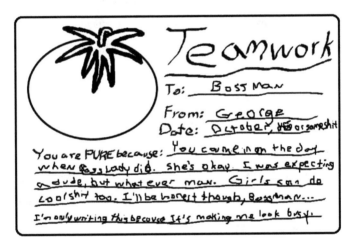

I gave the card back to George and he taped it on the wall. He then paced around for a bit, looking for something to do.

I circled around and started looking for Crabby, who strangely hadn't thrown the clipboard at me and left yet. After taking a few steps, I looked back. Something struck my attention on the schedule.

Wait... Why was Crabby crossed out for the day?

Instantly, I had my answer. From the back of the store, Janice treaded toward me... followed closely by Mitch, our district manager.

Oh, shit.

"So, bottom line," said Mitch, "I think your top three opportunities are Cleanliness, Recognition, and our P.U.R.E. Product. As a side note, our M.O.D. program is *the key tool* that needs to be utilized in order to achieve great efficiency with our with our team members. As it stands, Team Efficiency is *such an opportunity* that it's affecting our *Overall Guest Experience.*"

Dear God in heaven.

I made myself busy on the make-table while Janice tried to shoo him away.

"Just remember, everything that our guests can see has an impact on their experience," he said. "We need to embrace *P.U.R.E.* culture at this location. Really try to be positive. I'll be back in stores next week. If you need anything, you can always utilize your Everyday Business Binder."

Call me? No! Use your goddamn binder!

"Alright," said Janice.

She walked him out the exit. As I thought about it more though, this whole shebang really asked more questions than it answered. Did she *want* to walk the store with Mitch? Was she trying to protect Crabby? Or... maybe she just didn't want Mitch to *see* Crabby. But even then... *why?*

Janice walked back. Man, she looked beat. Her brand new shirt was stained with fryer grease and her eyelids weighed down on her like a pony carrying a three-hundred pound eight-year-old.

"That bad, huh?" I asked.

She had no words. She lifted her head enough to nod and walked behind me to show me the clipboard.

"To give you the quick rundown," she said, "I had two call-ins, register one stopped working, the oven shut itself off in the middle of the morning rush, and just when I got the oven working again there was a twenty pizza delivery order addressed to a business that no longer existed. Of course we only found that out when a driver made it to the empty building... which is when Mitch came in."

"Ouch," I said. "You alright?"

She gave me the clipboard and nodded.

"Don't worry, I got it," I told her. "Is register one working yet?"

She nodded.

"Awesome," I said. "I've got it from here. Have a good night!"

I jotted down a few notes about the schedule and wrote a reminder to fix Max's schedule.

"No...I can't leave," she said. "Crabby's going to be here in just a few minutes. We're going to have a quick manager meeting before I go. Also, can you help me out with something? I'm a little confused. How many times is the schedule changed per week?"

"Umm, a lot," I told her. "Nearly every day."

"That explains a lot," she said.

"What do you mean?" I asked.

"So, the past two days, we've had this guy named... *Luca* on the schedule," she said. "I was planning on writing him up because he never showed."

She pointed to her notes. Flipping the pages on her clipboard, she dragged her finger across the schedule for the day before. The records for both days were remarkably detailed.

"But both days, this guy named... *George* came up and worked the shifts for him," she said. "At first, I thought maybe Luca might be sick and found someone to switch with him, but now I'm starting to think he doesn't even work here anymore."

It shocked me how bad Crabby was at communication. How in the *living hell* did that not come up?

Before I could respond, she peeked over my shoulder and saw George getting his next delivery ready.

"George!" she said, "hold up!"

"I'm already punched out for delivery, Miss Janice," he said, trying to be polite. "You want me to punch back in?"

"It will only take a second," she said.

I rushed up to stop her.

"Janice," I said, "don't worry. The schedule wasn't changed."

"What do you mean, BossMan?" George asked. "The schedule is *always* changing! Have you met the person *making* the schedule? Crabby wouldn't be able to make up her mind if someone offered her the choice of a *million dollars* or *Armageddon on VHS.*"

We both knew she'd choose Armageddon, but I had to keep focused.

Maybe if I could tell Janice the situation immediately, without beating around the bush, George wouldn't go on a long spiel about it.

"George *is* Luca," I said. "It's just a nickname. We just call him George."

Janice looked at me in silence as it finally clicked. George looked back and forth at both of us until he decided to continue assembling his delivery.

I made a relieved sigh.

The gears continued to turn for Janice, though.

"George," she said softly, but firmly, "why aren't you wearing Luca on your name-badge?"

Well... I tried.

George gently put his delivery bag down and turned back around. He licked his lips and thought about his words carefully.

"Miss Janice," he said, "I believe it was Shakespeare who posed the question, 'What's in a name?'"

"I'm sorry," said Janice, "we're not going to stop calling you George, but I'm going to have to remake your name-"

"-Well, after hundreds of years, we finally have an answer," he said. "Bullying! That's what's in a name!"

"George," said Janice, "There's no denying that you're committed to this, but I think it's best if you-"

"-Oh look!" George shouted, "It's *Luca Skywalka*"

"George," said Janice.

"Hey, Miss Janice! I found a telescope!" George announced, "you wanna take a *Luca?*"

"Enough," she said.

"And *after that,*" said George, "we can go smoke! In a *Luca* Bar!"

"Okay!" she shouted.

"*Hey,*" George whispered as he peered behind the counter, "*What's the company policy on setting up group reservations for holidays?*"

Janice opened her mouth to answer.

"I don't know!" shouted George, "why don't you *Luca* it

up?"

"*Alright!*" she shouted.

George finally calmed down. For what seemed like a small eternity they just stood there, glaring at each other.

As the Joker once said, this is what happens when an unstoppable force meets an immovable object.

"... I guess..." said Janice, "I guess I can make an exception. Just this time."

And the immovable object remains victorious.

"Thanks, Miss!" George said and grabbed his bag once again. He hummed cheerfully as he double checked the pizza and *punched out for the delivery.*

Janice paused, flabbergasted. Her eyes widened with uncertainty about what just happened.

"*I thought you already punched out,*" she said.

George started walking but stepped right back when he noticed the warning, "Have you called the new customer?" on the screen. He, without a second thought, clicked yes and turned toward the door.

"You called them back?" she asked.

"Eh," said George and looked at the computer screen. "Well, whatever. It doesn't matter."

He marched off—leaving the unflappable Janice *inarguably flapped.*

After just a few minutes, Crabby clocked in and sat down with Janice and me at table zero, a nice round table toward the doorway. Janice sipped her second fresh cup of coffee and sorted the freshly printed paperwork with the sales and percentages for the past couple of days.

"How are you, Crabby?" she asked. "I'm glad that you could join us. I bet you're happy to have an extra day off this week."

"Well, it's not *really* a day off—" said Crabby. Her words flooded from her lips like water from a collapsing dam, "—if I have to be here for *however long.*"

Janice put the coffee on the table, sighed, and stacked up a pile of papers. She grabbed the stapler from next to her and jabbed a few packets together, then passed them to us one by one.

"Alright," said Janice, trying to keep her nerves in check, "let's see if we can make this quick, then."

"Let's see," said Crabby.

"So, Crabby," she said, "when you opened yesterday, Juan's R.A.C.E. score was only eighty-three percent. The company goal is ninety-seven. How do you think we can improve that?"

R.A.C.E. (Routines for Accurate Completion of Excellence)

is used to classify Pizza Corp's make-table policies and how fast the cooks are. Pizza Corp always loves to put convoluted acronyms on things.

Crabby shrugged. "We're not going to improve it," she said. "We can tell Juan to move faster, but even if we have three cooks working with him, our scores are going to suck."

"Okay…" Janice said.

Essentially, corporate contrives these numbers by setting a target amount of time for making each pizza, which is forty-five seconds. Twenty for saucing the pizza, five for adding the first layer of cheese, ten for adding the toppings, and five for adding the last layer of cheese. The cook's R.A.C.E. score for the day is the percentage of pizzas that were completed within that timeframe.

Corporate also suggests that each pepperoni pizza have *exactly* forty-eight pepperonis. *During visits, they're not afraid to count them.*

She flipped through the paperwork and arrived at the numbers from the day before that. Crabby opened her mouth to speak, but Janice talked over her.

"Juan's scores on Sunday were slightly better," she said. "He was at eighty-nine percent. That night, when Max came in, she was actually at ninety-two, so she was close."

"Yeah," said Crabby. "*Like I said,* the cook doesn't change anything. It's our customers. If we get ten orders of one-topping pizzas, our scores will go up. If we get three bullshit orders of complicated pizzas, they'll go down."

Crabby was partially right—our system sucked giant monkey balls, but a fast cook *did* make a difference. Not a tremendous difference, but a difference.

"Okay, then," said Janice, "Well, the point still stands. None of our cooks have met their goal since this time last year."

"And… they won't," said Crabby.

Janice ignored her.

"Drivers are the same way," Janice said, no longer dividing her attention between Crabby and me. "On our D.R.I.V.E. charts, none of our drivers got more than ninety-one percent for the week."

D.R.I.V.E. stands for *Delivery Routines Involving Vehicular Excellence.* Yeah, no—*that's real.* Delivery percentages work the same as cooking percentages. The only difference is they're typically calculated by week, not by day. *Don't ask. I don't get why either.*

"Do you guys know how long it should take a driver to take a delivery?" she asked.

We both shook our heads. I was pretty sure I knew the answer, but I didn't want to say the wrong thing.

"The system allows up to twenty-two minutes for each

double," she said, "so that's six minutes from here to their first delivery, six minutes to their second delivery, six minutes back here, and two minutes for each interaction with each customer. If a driver takes a single delivery, he or she has fourteen minutes."

Yes. That's also a real thing. That's corporate's expectation. All of our policies, spreadsheets and computer programs are based off of those little bullshit goals.

"We're in the same boat on all sides of the store," said Janice. "All of our other percentages are just as low. So what does that tell you?"

We stayed silent.

"It says that from beginning to end of our product's journey, we need to speed up. The queue-line is full because we're not taking orders fast enough. After we take the orders, they're late because we aren't making pizzas fast enough. Then, when the pizza is finally delivered, it's cold because the drivers aren't getting there in time."

To an extent, this was true. But, there was still a great deal that was out of our control. On the driver's side, construction. On the cook's side, big, complex orders. On the register, slow customers. Not to mention the amount of time that everyone spent doing things that weren't their job, like cut-table and tossing wings. Those numbers worked for a small few locations, I'm sure. However, they had extraordinarily average sales, a somewhat intelligent customer base, and were all well-staffed. Say what you want about busy stores making their numbers, but in my experience every store manager running a store that doesn't meet those specific guidelines has to fudge their numbers and break rules. Or else the store just won't function.

As Janice talked about our store's numbers, a customer walked in and got in line. Juan didn't know how to use the register, so there was no one who could take care of her. I waited for a few moments to see if maybe a driver would come in, but no such luck. After a brief pause, I scooted my chair back and promptly stood up.

"I'll be right back," I said.

As I headed over toward the counter, the phone started to ring. Because, of course it would. Policy was to answer the phone before the customers in line, and with Janice there, I couldn't ignore it.

"Just one second, ma'am," I said, "I'll be right with you."

She shrugged and glared at me.

"Fine," she said under her breath. "It's not like I'm in a *hurry* or anything."

I ignored her and picked up the phone.

"Thanks for calling Pizza Corp," I said. "This is Tony, will this be delivery or carryout?"

"Oh, hey, Tony. This is Mike."

Well... *fuck.* I knew where this was going.

"Hey, what's up?" I asked and grabbed the clipboard from the other side of the counter.

"Hey... I'm sorry..." he said, "I have the stomach flu. I should be better by tomorrow, but I've been throwing up all day..."

Great.

"Are you scheduled to work tomorrow?" I asked.

He took a moment and thought about it.

"Well," he said, "No... but if you need me, I *guess—*"

That was it. I had an idea.

Alright, here we go. Mike was going to open tomorrow and Max was coming in tonight, which was great. That killed two birds with one stone. The problem was that Max didn't have anyone to watch Dominic, which meant she'd have to watch him while she was making pizzas. *Since she was going to be in the store anyway...* it wasn't exactly a problem. As long as I could keep her as my cook, we were fine. But I had a bad feeling about the whole thing.

I took the customer's order and sat back down at the table, only to hear Janice finishing her conversation.

"—which means everyone drives. Every*one* should be capable of doing every*thing*," she said.

Crabby looked toward me with a dismissive glare.

"Tony," said Janice, "let's catch you up."

Shit.

"During Mitch's visit today, he mentioned that we should be focusing on cross-training and cross-performing our team members," said Janice.

"Let me guess," I said, looking directly at Crabby, "we're putting Max on the road."

Crabby nodded and glared at Janice.

"Only until our D.R.I.V.E. times improve," said Janice. "We're also going to focus on bringing drivers inside and introducing them to the make-table until our R.A.C.E. scores increase."

Yeah, except that didn't make any friggin' sense. That's what corporate's default solution is, though. Cross-train everyone. *That solves everything.*

"...Okay," I said. "One question, though. Wouldn't keeping our *'Aces in Their Places'* improve our chances of improving? That's what I was taught in training, at least."

"Mitch believes that mixing things up could get our team members out of their comfort zone and improve their overall performance," she said. "Also, it would help introduce them to every piece of the Pizza Corp puzzle."

Yeah, that sounded like a Mitch answer.

"He said it was either *that* or start taking disciplinary action," said Janice.

Well, at least she was honest about it.

I kept my mouth shut and took an exhausted, worried sigh. I didn't know how long this was going to last, but after hearing it in black and white terminology, I tried to look at the positive side. Max had been a driver before, so she knew the drill. We'd had a few incidents before, but those were few and far between, so hopefully nothing would happen again.

A few more minutes went by and we wrapped the meeting up. Crabby and I scooted our chairs out and started to head back.

"Tony," Janice said, "there's one more thing I'd like to talk to you about."

I paused.

"Crabby, you're free to go. Have a good night!" she said.

Uh oh.

"So," Janice said, "Tony, where do you see yourself going with the company?"

I didn't know what to say.

"I guess I see myself here for a long, *long* time," I said. "Why do you ask?"

"Well," said Janice, "yesterday, I took some time to talk to each member of the team individually. As many of them as I could, at least."

I nodded slowly.

"I wanted to know more about what I was getting into. I wanted to know how this store could function with only two managers," she said. "From what I hear, you had to borrow managers from some other stores."

"Well," I said, "well, yeah. I mean, we had to. Otherwise, Crabby and I would have ended up working overtime."

Janice nodded and raised her eyebrow, as if she knew what actually ended up happening.

Corporate isn't fond of overtime, as you can imagine. In fact, when an employee gets overtime, it's usually punishable by a write up or even termination. Overtime at Pizza Corp is a big, *big* deal. What's frowned upon even more, though, is working off the clock—*which I had to do a lot.* Sometimes there was no other choice. If Mitch had walked in during a rush on nearly any of the days that I was scheduled off, I no doubt would have been fired. Right there, on the spot. He then would have called a salaried manager to run the store in my absence.

"During those days, were there times when the manager

that you borrowed… never showed up?" Janice asked.

Well, fuck. She knew. Yep. She definitely knew. My secret was out like a baby's belly button.

"… Yeah," I said. "I mean… yeah."

"So…" she said, "when that happened, who came in to replace them?"

I sighed and resigned myself to the whole thing, much to my disdain.

"*I did.*" I told her, "I… well, I had to."

"That's what I've heard," she said.

Wait, what?

"I asked all of your team members who they came to when they had a problem, when they were unsure about something, or when there was a scheduling conflict," she said. "Unanimously, everyone said you."

"Well," I said, "I try my best."

"No, I think it's more than that. I think you've really stepped up," said Janice. "The biggest opportunity that Mitch covered during our visit today was staffing, but not just for team members. We need one more manager, a salaried assistant manager. Now, yesterday I took a fair amount of time to look at prior reviews. You've been recommended for a promotion numerous times. Did you know that?"

I slowly and suspiciously shook my head no.

She gave me a second to process what she had just told me, then continued.

"During the visit, Mitch's recommendation was just to write you and Crabby up until we could let you go and start with a fresh team," she said. "Off the record, I think that's the dumbest idea I've ever heard. So instead, I convinced him to let you go to MAPP"

Yes, more acronyms. Manager Assessment and Placement Program. It's exactly what it sounds like.

"I was wondering if you're interested," she said.

I nodded and thought about what to say, with no luck.

"Awesome," she said, "so, here's what I need from you. Keep your numbers up. Make sure your P.A.C.E., R.A.C.E. and D.R.I.V.E. scores are as great as they can be. Stay. On. *Top of it.* Switch the roles up. If you're working with a cook or cashier who can drive, send him or her on the road. Lastly, try your best to stay clear of customer complaints. It's going to take a lot to make this work."

I continued to nod. This was going to be a chore, I just knew it. The microscope was on me now. I didn't know how I was going to make this work, but I knew I needed to figure it out. Not just for my family, but for myself.

"Lastly," she said, "we need to pinpoint who your replacement is going to be."

"Wait," I said, "my replacement?"

"It's better to promote internally than hire externally," she said, "Although Mitch has his own ideas of what we should do, I know it's better to have a replacement ready for your position. Just in case he can't find another shift manager in time. It's not a guarantee that he or she will move up, but it will help *your* chances."

I thought about it as thoroughly as I could. This might just be exactly what I was looking for. If I could move up, not only would that give me more power in the store to fix all of its problems, but if I found my replacement, it would make for a much less stressful work environment. What's more, I might actually be able to support my family with an assistant manager's salary.

"Do you have an idea of who that would be?" said Janice.

I had more than an idea. With all certainty, I knew who I wanted as my replacement.

"I think so," I said, with a slight stutter.

"Who?" she asked.

"Max," I said, "I'm choosing Max."

"Thank you for helping me out," said Max, "I know I'm a

little hard to deal with..."

She sat Dominic down in the booth in the back corner, far away from anywhere the typical customer would eat. Janice was long gone by this point and the rush was starting to build up. Burt had clocked in just a few minutes before, and looking back, I could tell that he was handling it. Juan had left when Burt arrived, so I only had a few minutes before it would start getting out of control. I had to take some time to help Dominic get acquainted, though, and I especially needed to talk to Max about what had happened during the meeting.

"You're good, trust me. I've got you," I said, "but... there's something I need to tell you."

Plopping the backpack on the ground, she dug through and pulled out a brownie inside of a paper towel. After opening it up and showing Dominic, she sat it a few tables down from him. He started to get antsy.

"Mom—*Mommy*..." he said and started bouncing in his seat, "Mommy, food!"

Max grabbed a plastic bag and pulled a half-sandwich from it. She rustled in the backpack some more and grabbed his sippy cup with a bottle of soda and sat them on the table in front of him. She unscrewed the lid for him and pulled his legs down into the seat.

"Honey," she said.

Dominic wasn't having it. He wanted that damn brownie. He kicked, screamed, and tried to stand up, but Max once again pulled him back in his seat.

"*Honey!*" she said.

He still wasn't happy. He sprung to his feet again and held his arms toward his treat a few tables down. Max sighed and grabbed it.

"Dominic," she said in a firm, yet sweet voice that only a mother could make. Seeing his mother hold the brownie made him calm down a little bit.

"Sit down," she said. He slowly eased his butt in the seat and crossed his legs, gazing at the brownie with puppy dog eyes.

"Okay," she said, "you can eat the brownie…"

He reached out his arms and shouted, "*Thank you!*"

"Yes, you're welcome," said Max, "after you eat your sandwich."

His eyes dropped and turned toward the ham sandwich that rested on the plastic bag in front of him.

"Okay?" said Max.

Dominic dropped his head and loosely grabbed the sandwich with both hands.

"*Okay…*" he said.

"Max," I said, "I have to tell you something."

"What's that?" she asked as she meddled a bit more with

Dominic's bag.

"Janice called a manager meeting today," I said. "I don't know how to say this, so I figure I'll just say it."

"What is it?" she asked and looked toward me.

"Janice wants to try and promote me to assistant manager," I said.

"Oh," she said, "Tony... Tony, that's great!"

Then I could tell her the real news.

"You're my replacement," I said.

Her eyes hit mine like a train, stopping my breath completely. Nearly dropping the stack of diapers that she held in her hand, she continued to probe the expression on my face in disbelief. Her thumbs started to tap the bag, and continued faster and faster while she thought through what I had just told her.

"What?" she asked. "Are you... *are you for real?*"

I nodded.

"What..." she said, "what do I have to do?"

I sighed.

"Well, that brings me to the bad news," I told her, "During Mitch's visit, he decided that everyone who has a car needs to drive."

She shook her head and lifted her shoulders.

"Okay," she said, "I mean, *whatever!* I'll do it. That's it?"

"Are you sure?" I asked. "I mean, that's not entirely it. But that's the worst part. To tell the truth, I don't really know much more than that."

"Of course I'm sure," she said. She made a proud grin, a face I hadn't seen from her in entirely too long, and looked me square in the eye, "It's my job."

She stood up tall and stepped toward me. That was one of the things I loved about Max. Not only loved, but truly respected. She had gone through a lot. Every day was a challenge for her, but she knew that she had a job to do. It wasn't ideal, but she knew that she had to get back on her feet, whatever it took.

I pushed my worry aside and nodded.

"Alright," I said.

She bent down toward Dominic and kissed his forehead.

"Can you watch him for me?" she asked.

"Of course I can," I told her and started to explain to both of us why that decision made sense. "I've got Burt on the make-table tonight, and you know, it's only Tuesday. It's not going to be *that* busy, right?"

She sighed.

She was definitely confident but clearly nervous, and so was I. This wasn't the first time Dominic had been in the store during her shift and I was sure it wouldn't be the last, but usually Max was able to stay inside and cook. Dominic never needed too much attention, though. He was always able to keep himself occupied. He was a good kid.

"Okay, sweetie," Max told him, "Mommy's going to go to work, okay?"

Dominic continued to look toward the brownie and munch on his food, paying no attention to anything she was saying.

"Dominic," she said.

Still nothing. After a few seconds, she dug through his backpack and pulled out his Darth Vader toy, which immediately stole his attention.

"Okay, Dominic," she said, "I'm going to go to work, okay? You be good."

She handed him the toy and kissed his forehead again. Bending over, she gave him a hug that nearly knocked the toy from his hand. I could tell he was aggravated by it, but Max held herself there for as long as he let her before standing back up.

"It's supposed to rain tonight," said Max. "Do we have anyone else coming in?"

I shook my head.

I hate the rain. It attracts customers like a moth to a flame. I don't know what it is about it, but business always nearly triples during thunderstorms. When you factor in how nasty the roads are, it doesn't add up well for business. Or drivers.

"If it gets too crazy, I'll pull you back inside," I told her. "You know, you still have a chance to change your mind."

"No," she said, "I've gotta do what I've gotta do."

She gave Dominic one last hug.

"I love you," she told him.

"Love you too," he said and spotted the brownie again. As Max and I started walking to the front of the store, he reached for his sandwich once again and started nibbling on it.

He picked up Darth Vader with the other hand and started to ramble incomprehensibly. After a few moments, he looked back and saw her picking up her delivery bag.

"I love you too," he said again. He grinned to Darth Vader and spoke to him, "I love my mommy."

Max went around the counter and kissed Dominic on the cheek as she left through the front door. I started to wipe down the cut-table and prepared for the rush when I heard the rumble of the storm approaching, followed by the gentle patter of rain.

I had a bad, bad feeling about this.

"Next please!" I shouted.

Dozens of customers waited in the line with devastating indignation in their eyes. Their heart-piercing glares aimed at me bounced from my forehead and glided smoothly back to them in the form of an optimistic, customer oriented attitude.

Kill them with kindness, they say.

I looked at Dominic once more to make sure he was alright... and alas, he was. He just sat there playing with his Star Wars figurines and Barbie dolls. From the looks of it, Ken and Darth Vader were fighting over who loved Leia and Barbie more, but I couldn't tell. Barbie had Vader's lightsaber and Ken had Luke's. Darth Vader just bounced back and forth laughing about something. I don't know, maybe they were fighting about something else. Maybe Leia kidnapped Barbie and Darth Vader was helping her? Either way, it was adorable. After he finished, he looked toward the brownie a few tables down and started slowly munching on his sandwich.

The man in the front stood with his son, showing him something on his smartphone. The boy was enthralled, sure, but he should have chosen a better time and place—either that, or paid more attention to where he was in line.

I looked back toward Burt, who was completely swamped. He already had about fifteen orders stacked up, and most of them were more than three items. All of them included at least one pepperoni pizza. At this point, I didn't know what to tell the customers in the lobby in terms of how long it would take. Corporate policy was to keep the "Promise Time" below twenty minutes, even if it was going to take longer.

The man at the front of the line continued to pay no mind.

This happens a lot. I figured he was just distracted and probably didn't hear me the first time.

"Next customer, please!"

He looked toward me, squinted his eyes, and gave me a penetrating glare. He grabbed his son's arm as tight as he could, yanked him forward, and pulled and pulled, nearly dragging him until they ended up at the register. The kid was more than willing to go, but the dad continued to pull his arm anyway to prove a point.

"Whad'ya want, huh?" he asked. "*What did you want?* Did you want me to just—*just*... just run over here and *jump over the counter?* Is *that* what you wanted?"

Every once in a while in the service industry, you get a customer that you just don't understand. You get asked questions that you just don't have a clue how to respond to. Sometimes, you don't even know what it means. On top of that, you *have* to be nice to them. *You have to be.* Not only do you have to worry about setting them off just in case they're a psychopath hiding a gun, but there's also the chance that there are secret shoppers around. To them, it doesn't matter how rude a customer is. If you're not polite, it goes to corporate. The last thing I needed was a customer service complaint, especially if I was in the running for assistant manager and Max was my replacement. That would be the quickest way to ruin it for both of us.

"I'm sorry, sir," I said, "I don't quite understand-"

"-Did. *You.* Want. *Me*," he said, "to *run over here* and *jump over the counter*?!"

He groaned and stomped his foot.

"Aren't you listening?!" he said. "It's plain English!"

"Oh," I said, "my apologies sir."

It started to dawn on me. I thought I might have known what he meant.

"I'm sorry, sir. I thought you didn't hear me the first time I asked," I said. "It can be hard to hear with the oven-"

"No!" he said. "Do we look like we're from Mexico, or China, or—or *goddamn* South Africa!? *We speak the language!*"

What?

"You're right sir," I told him. "I'm sorry about all of that. Is there anything I can get started for you?"

He slapped a piece of paper on the counter and violently pushed it toward me. It started falling from my side of the counter when I plucked it out of the air. I unfolded it and started to read… it was an order of *twenty seven pizzas.* All with ridiculously specific toppings. *Well… fuck me.*

"How long?" he asked.

I took a second to skim through the order, much to his distaste, and started to type it in. I had no idea what to say. The wait time for a small order was about thirty to forty-five minutes. I couldn't imagine how long his order would take, let alone the orders for the people behind him. I thought about rushing through the line and typing each order in, then hopping on the make-table for just his order and his alone... but then I realized that everyone who ordered first would start to get pissy if his came out first. There really just wasn't a right way to do this. The best thing to do was just tell him the truth and try my best.

"This is a big order," I told him. "We'll go as fast as we can, but I think it might be about an hour before we can get it ready."

He grunted and looked toward the screen, which was completely full.

"It says carryout orders will be ready in twenty minutes," he said.

As you've probably gathered, it says that because we're not allowed to raise it up any higher. If we do, we get flagged. That's instant corporate attention and not the good kind.

"That's true, sir." I said. "But it's really, just... we really can't make an order this large in twenty minutes."

It was true. Not even on a slow day could we make an order like that in twenty minutes.

He plucked his phone from his son and started typing on it.

"Alright," he said, "but I hope you know that Mitch is going to have a pretty nasty email when he gets to work in the morning.

I've talked to him a few times before. He gets answers. Knows how to make the customer happy. I like him."

Fucking asshole. He's been around the block before. Not only does he know how to play the system, but he knows who to talk to and what to say. It makes me wonder how many times he's done this and who he's gotten fired.

"Yes sir," I said, "I understand. We'll have it out as fast as we can."

I started typing in the order as quickly as I could. I knew I needed to get over there and help Burt if this was going to work. As I clicked the pizzas in, he started whispering to his son once again.

"Hey. *Dallas,*" he said, "you know when he was all rushing us over here?"

His son nodded and grabbed his arm in remembrance.

"Well, next time he does that, I'm just gonna run up and leap over the counter. Then, just when he least expects it, I'm going to show him *who's* ordering *who* around," he said and gave the boy a soft punch, "Bam!"

"Wait," he said and stared at his vibrating phone, "I think you're mom wants beef instead of ham on her Hawaiian."

I paused and waited for him to figure it out.

He typed on his phone for a few more seconds, but stopped when he looked toward me.

"You look busy," he said.

"No worries," I said, trying my damnedest to be nice, "was there a change on the order? I can fix it."

He pushed out his bottom lip and gave me a stern glare.

"Does it look like there's any change?" he asked, and shook his head. "Don't you think I would tell you if there was?"

He leaned his upper body over the counter and pulled his face toward mine.

"Why aren't you doing anything?" he asked. "Type in the order."

At this point, I was more pissed than intimidated. I acted as though I was doing as he commanded to ease his anger, but all I wanted in that moment was to carve his eye out with a plastic spoon. He was so lucky that Janice was working here, so lucky that my wife had cancer, so lucky that Max's son was waiting for his mother in the lobby. He came into the store at just the right time. I thought to myself about how fortunate this guy was that all this hadn't happened two years earlier. If it had, I probably would have gotten fired… and it wouldn't have been from a complaint.

Regardless of how untrue that thought process was, it kept me calm enough to keep going.

"What do you need?!" I asked Burt.

The pizzas flew from our hands. We were booking it. Seventeen pizzas down, only ten more to go. Then, of course, the orders of all twelve people behind them. All of whom were pacing around the lobby, cursing and complaining about how long we were taking. The entire store looked like a mosh pit at a rock concert. Their footsteps shook the walls and their garbage rocketed in the air like a tornado hitting a landfill. The only tranquility was Dominic's table, which fortunately was the one thing that the customers stayed clear from. It was hard to see him from behind the make-table, but I popped my head up every few seconds to make sure no one bothered him.

"Pan-Meat-Lovers, Stuffed-Hawaiian, Hand-Tossed-Cheese!" said Burt, "and... and-shit!"

"It's all shit!" I said. "What do you need!"

Burt quickly wiped his hands on his shirt and pointed toward the M.O.D. screen that hung from the ceiling, which formerly only showed the cook and driver percentages for the night and had absolutely no use during a rush. At that moment, however, it beeped, buzzed, and flashed a red highlight across the screen.

"That *fucking thing!*" said Burt. "I'm gonna kick its ass! It needs to shut the hell up right now or I'm going to fuckin-!"

"Hold on, now!" I told him. "Let's see what it wants!"

I hopped off the make-table and sprinted over to get a closer look. The beeps pierced my ears. The flashing lights gave me a headache and made me grateful that none of our employees had epilepsy. It was hard to read anything that it was saying, even up close. I had to take a few moments to calm down and really concentrate before I got it.

"Burt!" I said, "check the cooler on the right!"

He tossed the pizza that he was working on into the oven and opened up the fridge. He did a quick count, looked at all the toppings, and paused after another few moments.

"What am I looking for?" he asked.

"It says..." I said, second guessing myself, "I think it's saying we're out of stuffed crust!"

Burt paused.

"Yeah!" he said, "we were *almost* out of stuffed crust. Then I made *some more!*"

"How did it know that?!" I asked.

"You got me!" he said. "That never happened before! You'd figure that if it knows we were out before, that it would know when we make some more!"

I didn't know how it worked. I had never messed with this screen before. Janice must have done something to it. I could see why. That feature would be super useful once we learned how to use it, but the fact was, we didn't. I had no earthly idea how to turn that fucking thing off.

"Well…" I said, "shit."

"It's all shit!" said Burt.

"You got that right," I said and looked around, "It's *all* shit."

Burt went back to the pizzas on the line and started topping them. After peering back and forth toward the noisy, flashing screen, he scraped the cheese and meat from his hands and pulled out his earphones and started listening to music. I guess that fixed his problem.

The driver door flew open, loudly hitting the wall. George ran in, and clocked back in from his driver's time.

"I don't think it's *gloomy* and *shitty* enough outside, BossMan," he said.

"Why do you say that?" I asked.

"Look at it," he said.

I looked out the lobby windows. It was horrific. I could barely see anything except for a nearby tree, which I instantly became worried was going to fall on one of the customers' cars. Was there a fucking tornado going on?

"I see," I said.

I looked toward the screen on the ceiling and tried to do some quick math. The average driver score was way, way off. Worse than usual, even considering the weather. It shocked me, and caused a small panic when I realized why. The drivers were timely. I had been watching every driver check in and out. They were all moving quickly. Every driver went out and back for no more than fifteen minutes at a time. Every driver, that is, except for Max.

I hadn't seen Max in over an hour.

"Is someone going to check me out?!" shouted a lady in the lobby.

She stood toward the middle of the queue line. It was a wonder how she thought we would even see her, much less think she was ready. I ran up to the counter and started to log in to the register but before I could say anything, in the corner of my eye, I noticed some high school jocks heading toward Dominic's table.

"How can I help you?" I asked, trying to stay focused on Dominic.

Her eyes, like fire, burned through mine like a laser beam. Her tone was soft and quiet, but vehement and fierce.

"I need to speak with your manager," she said.

"The store manager's not here," I said, "but I'm the manager on-"

"I. Don't. Care," She said, "I need to talk to your supervisor. Let me talk to someone. I've been waiting for twenty minutes. The service here is abysmal. And not only that, *but have you been in the women's restroom?"*

No. I absolutely have not been in the woman's restroom.

Dominic sat quietly and patiently looked toward his brownie. He was almost done with his sandwich. By this point, he'd given up on Darth Vader and Barbie and was more concerned with finishing his food so he could eat dessert. Loudly, the jocks barked about something I couldn't quite understand and threw their letter jackets on the tables next to him. This was bad.

"I'm sorry about that ma'am," I told her. "I'm the manager on-"

"-Just stop talking," she said. "Where's the manager on duty?"

One of the jocks pulled out a portable speaker and started blasting his music. The tallest jock, however, stayed pretty calm and reached toward the Darth Vader figurine.

"Who's that?" the jock asked and pointed to it.

Dominic's eyes lit up.

"Darth Vader!" he said and smiled, "*my* Darth Vader."

"Oh," said the jock, "it's *your* Darth Vader."

"Yes." Dominic clarified.

Dominic pointed toward the glass door next to him.

"My mommy," he said and mumbled something incomprehensible. "That door. *My* mommy."

The lady slammed her fist on the counter, grabbed the POS screen, and violently jiggled it. She scoffed, and pulled out her purse.

"You're not even paying attention," she said.

When she said that, I froze. I couldn't do everything. I knew I couldn't. I didn't know what to do. Every customer in the store was on the verge of causing a riot. Looking back into the kitchen, the cut-table was so backed up that pizzas were clogging and burning halfway through the oven. Burt needed my help making pizzas, which made me think about the guy waiting for his huge order, which made me wonder where Max was. Worrying about Max made me worry about Dominic and seeing Dominic made me think about the lady at the counter, which cycled back to Burt again. What *in the hell* was I supposed to do?

"Well," she said, "whenever you feel like working, there's vomit all over the ladies' room."

God dammit, as if I needed something else to worry about.

"Look. Just cancel my order. I don't care anymore," she said and picked up her purse and walked away. As she disappeared into the crowd, I was just left standing there, completely unsure of what to do next.

As the customers stared at me, they began to get louder and louder.

"You need more checkers!" one said, as if I could just spawn someone out of thin air. The man with his son was starting to get impatient, too. He pulled out his phone and started to shout about how much time I had left to finish his order. The jocks at the table started joining in with the jock who was talking with Dominic.

I took a minute to process everything and I finally came to a reasonable and managerial conclusion: *These assholes can fuck themselves.*

I rushed into the maintenance closet and started filling the mop bucket. I couldn't send the jocks away because there was still the off chance that they were just playing with Dominic, but I could start mopping the floor. The women's restroom was on the same side of the building as Dominic and cleaning up vomit was the perfect excuse to watch him. It sucked for Burt and I knew the customers would be pissed, but I figured it was the right thing to do. I just hoped that there was enough bile to last until they left.

Leaving it only about halfway full, I pulled the bucket over to the restroom and knocked on the door. No response. I went inside, made sure that I had a clear view of Dominic, and started mopping. The smell alone was disgusting and the vomit was dense. It was also far, far away from the toilet. It was like they did it that way on purpose. This wasn't my first rodeo, so it was pretty obvious to me when they were trying to make it to the toilet. There was usually a trail, or something. This time, it was as if they made it in the restroom and figured, "Eh. Oh well. Close enough."

The jock grabbed the Darth Vader toy with Dominic's permission. I felt a little relieved when I saw that.

"Luke," said the jock and made some breathing sounds, "I am your father."

Dominic laughed and reached out for it.

"My turn," said Dominic. The jock nodded and gave it back to him.

I was still on my last nerve, but it calmed me to know that he meant no harm. Dominic continued to laugh and play with him. The other jocks continued to blast their music and make crude jokes, but the one talking to Dominic stayed calm and gentle. As I cleaned, I saw another crowd of six or seven people enter and line up at the counter. I sighed, and decided that I needed to go back into the storm, even though I was perfectly content cleaning the vomit.

One of the ladies from the group walked toward me as I pulled the mop bucket out of the bathroom and let the door shut.

"Um," she said and looked back at the counter, "shouldn't you wait *until you're closed* to mop the floor?"

I hated these people.

"I'm sorry, ma'am," I said, "did you need to use the ladies' room?"

She grunted.

"Well, yeah! Why *else* would I be walking to the restroom?!"
she said.

I checked back up on Dominic, who was fine. I then looked
back toward the restroom and peered back at her. I'd been taking
my sweet time and hadn't hardly touched the vomit. It was still
everywhere. And it was nearly impossible to walk in without
stepping in it.

Trying my best to hold back a grin, I popped my hands off
the mop.

"Okay." I said, "you're right! I'm not sure what I was
thinking."

I paced back toward the kitchen and heard the door squeak
open behind me. Her hand stopped the door from closing as she
was forced to make the choice between being surrounded by bile
and bruising her pride. After she spent a good while thinking
about it, she tip-toed inside and let the door shut behind her...
It was *fantastic.*

Burt moved at warp speed. He was tossing pizzas into the
oven, cutting the burnt pizzas at the cut-table, boxing them, and

bouncing over to the wing-station and back with ease. I could tell he saw the customers trying to talk to him, but he not only couldn't hear them with his headphones turned all the way up, he didn't care. As I made my way behind the counter, I felt like I was being flung from the frying pan and into the fire. However, inside the fire, I had a newfound sense of optimism. The fire was warm, rudimentary, and completely absent of grease burns.

I quickly took their orders, one by one, and helped Burt on make-table. With only three orders to go, we started rocking and rolling. After throwing a few orders into the oven, though, I looked toward the kitchen clock. It had been nearly two hours since Max was in the store. I was starting to get worried.

Another half-hour passed by and we started slowing down. The big orders were finished, and all of the incomplete ones were in the oven. Regardless of how calm the kitchen was, though, the lobby was still packed like sardines in a can. The man with the twenty-seven piece order was on his way, but most others were in the middle of eating. We still had quite a ways to go before the night was over. I popped around the counter and grabbed the mop bucket. After checking out the mess, which was unbearable, I passed Dominic, who was still playing with his new friend.

Propping open the bathroom door, I noticed something that completely restored my faith in humanity... at least, what was left of it. The floor was clean. I had to double-take to make sure, but there it was. I didn't know who cleaned it, but whoever it was didn't take credit for it. I wished I could thank that Good Samaritan, but I figured chances were, he or she was already gone... As I walked back, I tried my best to quietly but alacritously express my relief just in case they were watching.

I walked back into the kitchen to further inspect the mess. Both wing-station tables were covered with frying grease, and the cut-table was littered with scraps, garbage, and broken boxes. Toward the back, there were three industrial size garbage cans filled with dishes, and toward the front the floor was completely black from the mud that the drivers were trailing in. Even with non-slip shoes, it was hard to stay balanced when I walked toward the driver-screen. I added to it the nearly unimaginable mess that was our lobby and the result I got wasn't fun to think about. We were going to be there all night. So much for saving labor.

Another half-hour passed. Still no Max. I tried calling her cellphone, but there was no answer. In the lobby, I started cleaning up tables. The first table was so bad that I had to bring a trash bag with me, and it ended up filling it. I tossed the first bag over the counter and nabbed the second one from the customer garbage can. It was not like they were using it, anyway. As I walked back, the mother of the last litter of customers started bringing their trash toward it.

"Just a second," I said. "Sorry, I took the bag."

She kept walking, paying no attention. Her kids and husband were still at the table, talking and drinking the last of their soda. She probably was just having a hard time concentrating.

"Ma'am," I said and raced toward her, "excuse me, ma'am."

Making it to the trash can, she looked inside and debated for a second before throwing the garbage in. It was only just when she finished tossing the last bit when she turned around and noticed me standing there. I tried not to look upset about it. I tried, though I'm sure I had the face of a heartbroken puppy. That was just the icing on the cake. I knew consciously that it wasn't much and cleaning it wouldn't take but a few minutes, but I felt like crying. That was all I needed... one more mess.

"Oh," she said.

We stared at each other for a good few seconds as we both thought about what to say next.

"Well," she said and let out a nervous chuckle, "it's job security."

I stared at her for just a little longer. This time, completely expressionless. Numb in every sense of the word.

"Yes," I said. "Thank you, ma'am. I hope you have a good night."

As she rounded up her husband and kids, I grabbed some gloves and scooped their scraps from the bottom of the can and put it into the bag. I guess, on some level, I did that to myself. The family left, leaving only a few customers in the lobby, and the jocks finally turned their music off. My ears were filled with a high-pitched buzzing, which felt like the complete absence of sound. With the exception of a splitting headache, the store was finally quiet.

"Hey. Tony," said Burt from behind the counter.

I sat on the floor, motionless. Whatever it was that he was going to say, I just didn't care anymore. All I wanted to do was sit there.

"Tony," said Burt.

I got up and dusted myself off. Without saying anything, I raised my eyebrows and lifted my head as if to tell him that I was paying attention.

"Oh hey," said Burt, "I'm going to take a shit. Be back in a second."

I flung my hand skyward and made a sarcastic thumbs-up. Giving him a sardonic grin, I turned around and plopped back down in my pile of trash. I heard Burt march behind me into the restroom, and I told myself that he had the right idea. I leaned my head on the garbage can and convinced myself that I could relax for a just a minute.

That was, until I heard Dominic scream from behind me.

"Dude! What are you doing?!" shouted the leader jock.

Dominic bounced and wrestled with him, reaching out for his brownie that one of the other guys was holding. His eyes watered, and he stomped his legs rapidly.

"*Mommy food!*" he shouted and pointed as his empty plate, "*Mommy! My mommy food!*"

I shot to my feet, just as the phone started ringing— of *fucking course*. I didn't want to get it. I should have let it ring and I knew it. I didn't want to talk to those *fucking* people and I knew that I should have devoted that time to figuring out what was happening with Dominic, but I couldn't do it. I had to answer it. Not just to save my own ass, but I knew that it could have been Max who was trying to call.

I darted to the phone and yanked it off the hook. I needed to make this as fast as possible if I was going to stop whatever was going on with Dominic.

"Thanks for calling Pizza Corp, this is Tony," I said. "Will this be for delivery or—"

The jocks started screaming at each other. I could hear them moving, but I couldn't tell where or how. Dominic screamed louder and louder, but his last cry was hampered, as if one of them was covering his mouth. I dropped the phone and leaped over the countertop. Why I thought that was a good idea, I'll never know. As I made my way down the other side, I tried to catch myself with my hands but the mud on the floor made them slip… and down I went. My cheek slammed into the tile and my knees crashed against the marble. I flipped once more and finally crashed on my back. I moved my knees as quickly as I could to get up, and they hardly budged. I crawled to the back of the nearest booth and pulled myself on my feet. I barely managed to stay there.

"Dude, just give him the damn brownie!" said the jock that held Dominic.

"What makes you say that it's his?!" shouted the jock with the speaker. "It was like, three tables away from him!"

"Come on, man!" said the leader. "He obviously wants it, just give it to him!"

He was holding Dominic tightly, unsuccessfully trying to keep him from screaming. Dominic pressed his chest into the jock's and tried desperately to pull his hand from his mouth. The jock's other hand pressed against Dominic's back and started putting pressure on it. Before I could even make a noise, Dominic's yelling started to be less and less a fight for his reward for eating his dinner. It increasingly became a howl of pain.

"Hey, asshole!" I shouted. "What the hell are you doing? Let him go!"

The phone started to ring again, but I didn't care. I touched my face and felt the blood that started gushing out of my swollen cheek. I was light headed and my vision started to go dark.

Dominic abruptly stopped crying. The jock that held him went quiet as well. His friends continued for a few minutes but dropped everything when they noticed what was going on. The leader squinted his eyes, and dropped his jaw. When he looked down toward Dominic, he made a disgusted grunt.

"Holy shit!" he shouted, "are you fucking serious?"

Feeling the warm dribble down his soaking jeans, he pushed Dominic away and bolted upward, backing away quickly. Dominic threw himself backward and his head crashed against the corner of the table. Flailing silently, he smashed facedown on the floor. I pushed myself away from the booth and bolted toward him.

I crawled under the table, sunk my hands under Dominic, and carefully pulled him out. Lifting him up slowly, I rested his head on my shoulder and massaged his back gently with my fingertips, checking for anything that seemed out of the ordinary. Within a few moments, Dominic took an enormous breath and let out a terrifying shriek.

The jock ran toward the counter and grabbed some paper towels. He wiped his drenched pants anxiously, as he waited to see if Dominic was alright. His friends pulled at his jacket, urging him to leave, too frightened to say anything. I continued to rub Dominic's back, but I couldn't feel anything strange aside from the scarring and scabs that were left over from his recent surgeries. I wasn't a doctor though. There was no way for me to tell.

I shooed the jocks away and tried my best to calm Dominic down. I reached toward the brownie and held it toward him. He pushed it away, but it seemed to ease his pain. After a few minutes, his shrieks and screams decreased to a quiet whimper. I gently pulled him to the side and checked our clothes. We were both soaked. It wasn't blood, thank God, but I knew he'd need a replacement outfit from his bag. Hopefully he had one. I made my way to both doors and locked them. We still had half an hour before we were supposed to close the lobby, but I didn't care anymore. If someone came up I'd let them in, but I wasn't about to let the lobby get flooded with them again.

The driver door slammed open again. George sprinted in and punched in for his delivery. He took a peek at the screen and looked around the store. Two deliveries on the screen, but none of them ready. He let out a long sigh and tossed his bag onto the shelf. As he walked over to the cut table, he bent down and looked into the oven. Nothing. He looked toward the make-table screen. Ten minutes overdue. Thanks, Burt.

He lifted his shoulders and started wiping the table.

"George!" I scorned.

He lifted his eyebrows and looked toward me. Focusing on my face, he lifted his pointed finger to his and waved it around.

"Whoa," he said, "who'd you punch?"

I took a breath and shook my head. I just... didn't even. My vision continued to blur, but I couldn't sit down while I was holding Dominic.

"Where. *The hell.* Is Max?!" I scolded, as if he knew.

He squinted his eyes.

"What do you mean, where's Max?" he asked.

I didn't know how to respond. I knew he was driving. He was out doing his job. None of this was his fault. Yelling at him felt good though, and I knew he could take it. He knew that I was just venting. All he ever did was just stand there and raise his eyebrows at me, pretending to care. Then, after I was done, he'd go back to what he was doing.

"What do you mean *what do I mean?*" I barely made out the words.

I continued to softly rub Dominic's back and he slowly stopped fussing. He lifted himself up and pointed to the brownie. He peered toward it and back to me as he started to squirm out of my arms.

"Hold on," said George, "she's not here?"

I struggled to hold Dominic.

Feeling dizzy, I knew I couldn't hold him much longer. I had to put him down. When I did, he ran to the brownie, which was crumpled and smashed on the floor. I ran over and beat him to it. Picking the largest piece up, I gave it to him and sat down on the chair.

"George," I said, "why would you think she's here?"

I started rubbing my head. Dominic shoved the piece into his mouth and sprinted back over to his dolls. He jumped on the chair with ease, started playing, and was quick to entertain himself again. It was a relief. It didn't guarantee he was alright, but at least he good for the moment.

"What do *you* mean?" asked George.

I gave him a silent stare.

He looked around the kitchen and back at me. It took him a few seconds to process what was going on.

"Well…" he said, "her car's parked outside."

The fuck?

I gathered my energy and sprinted as fast as I could out of the driver door, being extra careful not to slip again. There it was, Max's car.

The rain was pelting. It was almost unbearable. While I

stepped toward her car, the wind started to pick up and nearly knocked me over. I had to lift my hand over my face to block the rain from my eyes, but inside of her car I could see a dim light. I made it closer, and beneath the drenched windshield, I saw her there. In the car. Her face was as bad as mine. Cut, bruised, scratched, it looked like someone had hit her jaw with a baseball bat. I knocked on the window and opened the door.

"Hey... Max," I said. "Where did you go?"

The rain flooded into the car. It bombarded the steering wheel, the dashboard, everything. But she didn't budge. Her car looked fine, aside from the dents that it always had. She clearly hadn't been in an accident. She looked at me and reached out her battered hand. It was drenched, but not with rain. She bled into my palm as I grabbed it.

"What happened?" I asked her. "You alright?"

She shook her head.

"I'm..." she started. She couldn't look me in the eye, but she desperately tried to. "I'm so sorry."

"Hey," I said, "it's okay. Just tell me what happened."

I tried to pull her up, but she wouldn't move. She was perfectly content to sit there, drenched, bloody, and completely beat up in her flooded car.

"Come on," I told her, "we need to dry you off."

She sighed, and pulled her hand back.

"Were our numbers okay?" she asked.

They weren't. They were terrible. But I nodded anyway. With whatever it was that happened to her, she clearly didn't need this added to it.

"The numbers are fine… but that doesn't matter," I said. "Can you tell me what happened?"

She took a sigh of relief and gathered her thoughts.

"I took that last delivery to East Oak," she said, "and… after I gave him his pizza, he reached his arms out and tried to grab me."

I stayed silent, trying to listen to her.

"He didn't even pay for it," she said. "He just… reached out. He didn't even say anything."

"What happened next?" I asked.

"I pushed him away and tried to run," she said. "But he pulled my arm inside and I fell on his doorstep. I tried to get up, but… he slammed the door on my fingers… and he just… held me there."

She looked at her hands without moving them. They were red, swollen, and shaking uncontrollably.

… And then it hit me. Half of these customers were new. We didn't call him back—Max took a delivery *and I didn't call the customer back.*

I was the manager on duty… *I let this happen.*

"When he opened the door, I took off," she said. "I didn't look back... I had to scrape my hands from under the door..."

She smacked her head against the seat and closed her eyes.

"I can't..." she said, "I can't move my hands..."

I bent down on my knees and reached out my hand. He placed hers on mine and started to get up.

"Is your phone on silent?" I asked.

Shocked, she quickly searched the cabin of the car. After a moment of realization, she pulled her hand away, threw her head back once again and let out a quiet sob.

"It fell out of my pocket when I was running away," she said, "I felt it drop but didn't get it..."

She pulled her palms to her muddy face and just cried. She didn't care about my presence anymore. She just sat there, whimpering, letting it all out.

"Come on," I said and gently tugged her arm, "hey... let's get you patched up."

I pulled her out of the car and we started walking inside. As I turned around, I saw George behind me. He ran over to the door and held it open for us. Holding her arm over my shoulders, I helped her inside. As we passed George, he nudged my back to get my attention.

"Hey," he said, "can you reprint that ticket for me?"

I nodded and walked into the lobby to sat Max down next

to Dominic.

"Why do you need it?" I asked.

"I'm a *guy*. He's not going to grab *me*. And BossMan, trust me. I grew up in an area much worse than this," he said. "I'm gonna get her phone back."

Max huddled up to her son and pulled him into her lap.

"Tony," said George, as he clocked Max back in for her, "Do you want me to punch out for delivery?"

I shook my head no and walked back.

"Just be careful," I said.

Later on, I cashed the drivers out. George took the longest to get back, but he managed to retrieve Max's phone. The glass was shattered, but at least it was usable. Dominic had a fresh change of clothes and went fast to sleep around ten o'clock, and we didn't have any more deliveries before we closed at eleven. It took us hours, but we cleaned the store up. I let Reece and George go home around one o'clock in the morning and I stayed with Max until two. By that time, she could move her hands again and the swelling had started to go down. It took half of the store's bandages to patch her up.

At the end of the night, we just sat there in the booth.

Dominic rested his head on her legs and Max examined the bruises gently. I stayed a few feet away from her. I didn't want to be a bother, but I enjoyed her company and was relieved that they were both alright.

"I'm so sorry, Max," I told her. "This is all my fault."

She shook her head, but stayed quiet.

"I should've made you call the new customer. I shouldn't have made you drive tonight," I said. "I should have fought with Janice and told her that we need to keep you inside. And better yet, I should have just told you to stay home today."

"No. It was my fault. This was my choice," she said. "You can't help whatever decisions your bosses make. You were just doing your job. Every time you asked me, you always said that I could change my mind."

She pulled her fingers through Dominic's hair.

"I shouldn't have brought him to work again," she said. "I knew eventually something like this would happen."

She grabbed me by the arm and pulled me over to her, but I only scooted an inch or two. I still felt horrible. I couldn't believe I let this happen. I was the manager on duty. I was her boss. I was the person who was watching Dominic. I couldn't believe I let them down. This was all on my watch.

I looked toward her, and back toward the store. If this was going to work, something was going to have to change. This couldn't happen again. As she rubbed her bruising hands gently, she made the occasional flinch every time she hit a tender spot. I looked at them and wished I could have made it all go away. Bandages covered most of her gashed fingertips, soaking the blood that had just barely begun to stop flooding from her gaping wounds. Surrounding the bandages, her hands had lost all normal color. On the outside, they were blue and purple. On the inside, they were a deep, intense shade of brown.

"What are we going to do?" I asked.

She sighed. Without even looking at me, she continued to rub her hands. Dominic's eyes bounced open. He looked at me and quickly shut them again. Slowly, he opened his eyes toward Max and kept them open. As she flinched and let out a quiet but pained noise, Dominic abruptly pushed himself up and sat his hands on the table. He looked up and back down between Max's hands and his and thought about it for a second before rubbing his own hands together.

"Maybe if we tell Mitch—" I said.

Max shook her head.

Dominic scooted closer to her, reached one of his hands toward her thumb, and started to rub it the way she was rubbing her other fingers. She smiled at him and kept going. He thought about what he was doing a bit more, staring intently at her bruises, and eventually put his hands in his lap after she let out a few more painful groans.

"Mommy," he said, "it hurts?"

Max nodded.

"Yes," she said, "it hurts."

He flailed and bounced from her lap and darted toward the backpack, dodging our legs as he went by. Making it out from under the table, he jerked the zipper open and started digging around.

"What are we going to do?" I asked and let out a quiet sigh.

Max stayed silent.

"Mommy!" Dominic shouted as he grabbed a toy, hurtled himself back under the table and into her lap.

"Mommy, Mommy!" he said.

Pushing himself up, he placed Darth Vader on the table and as gently as possible pulled her hands apart. He used both hands to open her palm and rested his toy in her hand, then carefully wrapped her fingers back around it.

"Darth Vader," he said. "Here go. You feel better, Mommy."

She looked at Darth Vader and tightened her grip. Pulling her other hand toward her face, she rested her bruised head in her palm and rinsed out a few more tears. After dwelling on the uncertainty that lay before her, she took a breath and looked toward Dominic, who was still looking back at her.

"It's okay, Mommy," he said and wrapped his arms around

her chest, "I got you. You feel better."

She nodded.

"Yep," she said, "Mommy will feel better."

Dominic reached his hand over, forced her fingers away from his toy and started to rub them once again.

She wiped away the rest of her tears with her free hand, took another sigh, and looked back toward me with the same brave, strong eyes that she had six hours earlier. She had already made her decision.

"We won't win this war by seeking victory in every battle," she said. "We'll win by choosing the victorious ones."

"What?" I asked.

"We can't tell Janice," she said, "or anyone for that matter."

I looked back toward her and rubbed my swollen face.

"Why not?" I asked.

"If we tell her, she'll tell Mitch," she said, "and what would Mitch think?"

"It doesn't matter what he thinks," I said. "This can't happen. Not to you, not to anyone."

"Tony," she said and quietly impaled my entire wellbeing with one valiant gaze.

"*This will happen.* No matter what we do. And it *has* happened," she said. "You think one accident report is going to change that?"

"Well," I said, "what if we go through HR? Let's go up the chain. Someone has to listen—"

"—Tony," she said. "How many times do you think this has happened? Not just here, but anywhere. How many times do you think someone has gotten hurt at any store, any district, or any company?"

I paused.

"I... I don't know," I said.

She looked back down at her hands.

"Well, I don't either," she said, "but I promise it's happened."

I sighed.

"If we tell Mitch, not only will it *not* help anyone else, it's going to hurt us. We didn't call that guy back. It's on us," she said. "Look at it from Mitch's perspective. He's just doing his job. He's got a boss and his boss has a boss. Knowing this store, he's probably already dismissing us—he doesn't see us as capable enough for a promotion, only Janice does. His boss is most likely telling him to phase out the managers that won't cooperate with his policies anyway. If I'm going to make a fuss about doing *my* job, why would he consider me as a capable person for *someone else's job?*"

I looked toward Dominic, still rubbing her hand. I couldn't bear it. She was right. Janice said so herself. I didn't want to admit it, but it was true. We had to do what Mitch said.

"So..." I said, "where do we go from here?"

She took a long, quiet breath.

"You're the boss," she said. "You tell me."

"*Great, thanks,*" I told her and chuckled. "Way to be a team player."

She grinned and peered toward me.

"Hey now," she said. "I'm just putting my aces in their places."

"You can shut the fuck up," I said. "You kiss your mother with that mouth?"

I got her to laugh, which was nice. Even with everything that was happening, it was nice to know that we could still be comfortable with each other and just be ourselves.

"Okay, okay," she said. "For starters, is there a way to stop that guy from ordering any more pizzas?"

I nodded.

"It's going to take a few days," I said. "Corporate has a three-strike rule. I'm going to have to make two more orders for him and flag them. You're off tomorrow and the next day, at least. So, when you get back, we should be good."

She nodded and thought about it for a second.

"Even then, though, it will still be blocked by his phone number," she said. "There's nothing stopping him from using someone else's phone."

"True." I said, "We could start calling new customers back."

She laughed so hard she snorted… but I was completely serious.

"I thought we were trying to make our scores *better!*" she said. "We need something else. Can you imagine calling each of those people back?"

I sighed.

"We can worry about that later," I said, with full intention of doing so.

"At least it's a start," she said.

"Agreed," I said. "While I'm at it, I can ask Janice if I can take on more responsibilities. Maybe she'll let me make the schedule."

"Doesn't Crabby make it?" she asked.

"Yeah," I said, "but Crabby's not exactly standing on solid ground right now. If I can make the schedule, I can schedule you with me so you won't have to drive."

"That would be a nice change anyway," she said. "Maybe we can turn this defeat into a hidden victory."

I smiled.

Dominic paused in the silence between our voices. After looking at both of us, he made a grotesque growl and clutched Darth Vader again. Imitating the Dark Lord, he breathed heavily and slammed the toy on the table and started speaking for him in

125

gibberish. Max grinned toward him and stretched out her tense fingers, preparing them for use.

"Well, we probably have to go," she said, "It's late. He needs to be in bed."

Dominic paused.

"... No, mommy."

She glared back and nodded.

"Yes, mommy," she said, imitating him.

"Yeah..." I told her, "I need to get back home anyway."

She made an optimistic grin and pulled Dominic up. I turned all the lights off, locked all of the lobby doors, and checked off my list of closing duties.

After a few minutes, we made it to the exit only to find two Teamwork Tomatoes taped to the door at eye height.

This is what they looked like:

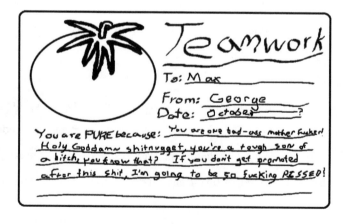

Thanks, George.

We made it out and locked the door behind us. We were soaked, wounded, and mentally drained. Although we felt as dead as a plank rotting in the autumn drizzle, our partnership remained victorious, strong and solemn—like a statue in a lightning storm.

Act 2

CHAPTER 4

This is what a traffic light looks like:

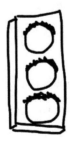

Traffic lights are hung on either wires or poles about thirty feet or so over street intersections. They're meant to advise drivers about when and where they should go. That's their one and only job. Like most humans, usually they don't completely suck at it.

This one did.

I was on my way to Pre-MAPP. As you could've guessed, that's another Pizza Corp acronym. MAPP stands for Manager Assessment and Promotion Program, but what it really means is Managerial Attention Possibility... Producer, or *whatever.* Sarcasm. It's pretty much a fancy name for a program that gets your district manager to actually pay some attention to you. Essentially, MAPP is a series of interviews followed by a tour with your DM. At the end of the day, your DM gives you a rating from one to five.

With Pizza Corp, however, any time anything is rated on that scale, it's taboo to use either one or five. One suggests that you are so bad that you can never improve, while five is unrealistically perfect. As a result, *(and this will be important later so keep it in your handy-dandy notebook),* MAPP is ranked in all actuality on a scale of two through four.

Luckily, according to Janice, Pre-MAPP doesn't really matter that much. I still didn't understand why Janice was sending me this early in the process, but she insisted that since she'd handpicked the store manager to interview me, it was going to be a guaranteed pass. On top of that, the manager would be honest with Janice about what I needed to learn before my meeting with Mitch. All I had to do was get there on time. Yeah. *So that's where we were.*

Ten minutes late. *Ten.* I hated myself. They probably thought that I was a no-show already. If I would've left ten minutes earlier, I would've been on time. I probably wouldn't have even gotten stuck at that light to begin with. I should have accounted more room for error. I needed to walk in and accept the consequences.

As I pulled up into a parking spot, I slammed my head on the steering wheel and marched in before I had time to overthink the situation. There wasn't but a single car in the lot, meaning all the drivers were out and there were no customers. This was a flagship store, which meant it had good numbers. The store manager I was supposed to interview with was probably twiddling his or her thumbs, just waiting for me to come in. Man, I felt like an idiot. As I opened the doors, all I heard was screaming. The entire staff was running around like chickens with their heads cut off, and I couldn't tell who was managing whom. It took some nerve, but I walked up to the counter and stood tall, waiting for someone to greet me.

Yeah. No one noticed.

I seriously doubted they would have heard me if I'd *shouted* at them. It made me wonder if the manager was going to notice my tardiness. Maybe this was my saving grace. I watched them scuffle and started to wonder how I was going to do this. The longer I stood there, the less I worried about being late and the more I worried about having the interview at all. Needless to say, it was pretty awkward. Every few seconds, there'd be a moment when someone wasn't blatantly yelling at someone else, and I'd try to say something, but just at that moment someone else would catch that opportunity and make a much bigger commotion than I could have ever made.

I nearly gave up, but when I looked down at the other end of the counter, where customers were supposed to line up, I noticed the bell duct-taped by the register. Right next to it was a piece of paper that was also taped on the counter. It was a handwritten, bold, and underlined letter asking the customers to, "PLZ RING BELL 4 SRVICE!1!one."

Someone had a sense of humor.

I didn't want to ring the bell. I knew what that bell meant— at least at my store, it meant that an impatient customer wanted his pizza. Or... it meant Dominic was playing with it. Either way,

I didn't want to start off acting like a three year old.

It started to look like there was no other way. I placed my hand over it and prepared for the ridicule that was about to come...

"Be right with you!" said one of the workers.

Man, that was close.

"I'm just here for Pre-MAPP," I said, although clearly none of them heard me.

After a few more minutes of tussling, one of the workers brushed the chicken wings off of her shirt and hurried up to the counter.

"Placing an order or picking up?" she asked.

"Oh. Um," I said, as she started to get testy, "I'm just here for Pre-MAPP."

She looked at me in the same way that I looked at everyone from behind the counter. It was a refreshing change of pace.

"So, are you picking up or..." she asked, and it clicked.

"Oh," she said, "you'll want to talk to Katty. She's our manager. It will be a few minutes. Go ahead and take a seat."

"No problem," I said, and wandered toward the closest booth. "Thanks!"

"You want something to eat?" she asked.

I peeked once again into the kitchen, looking at the mess.

"No thanks," I said, "I think I'm good."

She made an audible sigh of relief and marched back into the kitchen.

"Awesome!" she shouted, "she'll be right out!"

As I sat down, I listened to what they were saying in the kitchen and tried to understand their method. At just the moment there was a silence, the CSR yelled at the top of her lungs, "*KATTY!* There's a *GUY here for PRE-M.A.P.P!*"

Without missing a beat, I heard another voice yell right over her.

"I know, I know, I know!" she shouted, "*I know, I know, I know, I know!*"

The screaming continued for longer than you'd ever believe.

As I waited, I watched them intently. This was the flagship store of our district; I had to see how they managed to hit their numbers during the rush. Their formula was wildly off process, yet it seemed to have a process all of its own. Once the person at either make or cut-table got an order on the screen, they'd press the button saying that they'd completed the order, then the computer printed out the customer's receipt. The person at the cut-table gave the cook all of the receipts, then the cook would pass them back after he sent the order through the oven. The screens were left out entirely. No wonder they had such good scores. The drivers were all punched in and out manually, by Katty. It was like clockwork. At exactly fifteen minutes, she'd punch the driver back in and out on the next delivery. At my store, this would fail everywhere. We'd have declined credit cards, customers refusing to pay, cancellations at the last second, and a vast array of other problems. But here, the customers were all either businesses that were trying to cater or employees on their lunches. Every order was nearly identical, and they were all reliable. And... *there were no new customers.*

Trying to piece together how their customers could be so cooperative, I examined everyone who walked in to pick their orders up. There were very few. During that thirty minutes of waiting, they only had two carryout customers. Both were in uniform, and both were picking up large orders. After that first hour went by, it hit me. I knew the difference.

All of these customers were at work.

It seems like something that'd be easy to brush over, but it wasn't. That explained why they were just in and out. That was why they were in such a hurry. That was why the drivers didn't have any issues with their deliveries, and that was why none of them complained about getting low tips. The entirety of this store's clientele was businesses and grunt workers. They were all in a hurry because they needed to be. They knew how Pizza Corp worked because that's what helped them get their orders quicker. They were nice because they were in that customer service mindset. They were tipping because it wasn't their money to spend.

They, too, were customer service robots.

I waited for hours—I was *nerve-wrecked,* but I expected it. Every single interview I'd had with Pizza Corp was like this. When was at MAPP for my current position, it took *all day.* Even though I was scheduled off, I was interviewing from sunrise until sunset. For MAPP, even Pre-MAPP, you pretty much have to budget all damn day. I was lucky, I guess, that I had to go to work after. I had an excuse to cut it short if I needed to.

Katty was busy tossing wings, making pizzas, grabbing the phone, everything that she wasn't supposed to be doing, but she was doing it quickly. When it would slow down for a bit, she'd pick up the clipboard and start doing checklists, but she always found herself back on the make-table. Every time I thought it was over, another group of orders flooded in. I could only imagine how they felt, but I figured that this was a day to day routine for them. Just like Sunday nights at our store, or really any other night.

I cautiously pulled out my phone and checked it. I had just one text. It was from Trinity.

"You want anything from the store?" the message said.

"You're supposed to be in bed," I typed.

"Hey now," she replied, "I was advised to stand up for brief moments once every four to five hours."

"They didn't advise you to go to Walmart," I typed.

"I've been laying down for twelve hours!" she replied. "I've been saving up!"

I sent her a gif of Han Solo saying, "That's not how the force works!"

She sent, ":P"

"Just be careful," I typed.

I thought about it for a few moments.

"And yes. Get me some chocolate syrup," I typed.

Just as I put my phone back in my pocket, I heard a voice form behind me.

"Hey, Tony right?" she said. "I'm Katarina."

"Nice to meet you, Kat-" I started.

"—Yeah, that's what *my tag* says," she said. "Don't call me that. Mitch calls me that, but don't act like Mitch. The name's Katty. I trained Janice, she knows better. Pretty soon, you will too."

At least she had a sense of humor.

Hopefully that was humor.

One thing was for certain, though. This store was weird.

"Before we start, I gotta tell you…"

Before she could finish her sentence, she found a CSR walking slowly from a clean dishwasher. Without missing a beat, she snapped at him and he rushed to the make-table.

"Hey, Jonathan!" she shouted, then gave me a quiet nudge and pointed at the clipboard, "you had your *break* yet?!"

He paused, looked up at her, and quickly made his mind up to continue heading toward the cook's overwhelming stack of prep. Katty chuckled and snorted at him. He tried to ignore her and hid next to the cook and a few other workers who had no problem brushing it off.

"Eh, he'll come around eventually," she said. "He started a few days ago. He made the mistake of asking for a break, like, *thirty minutes* into his shift."

She shrugged and started talking under her breath.

"This is *Pizza Corp.* There are no breaks," she said. "It's part of the deal. You want a break, learn to drive. Nothing against the poor kid, but work is work. When you're here, you gotta be here. There's always something to do. He'll get the hang of it pretty soon. Either that, or he'll quit. One or the other."

Well, she wasn't wrong… and breaks were a subject that corporate was pretty dodgy about. If you brought it up, they'd get into a circular argument about how giving employees unpaid half-hour lunches instead could help save labor. Then, they'd follow that up by urging us to remember to try to staff as well as we could. Responses like that were corporate's standard arguments against morally ambiguous questions.

Most states have laws regulating breaks for retail employees, but fast food managed to slip passed them for whatever reason.

"Anyway," said Katty, "I feel the need to warn you that Janice sent you to this store for a reason."

I nodded slowly.

"I'm blunt, and I'm honest," she said. "I've done Pre-MAPP and MAPP for a lot of people, and it's not uncommon for me to say the wrong thing and *really* offend someone. I'm going to get under your skin. I'm probably going to hurt your feelings... but it'll make you better. You get me?"

Oh, yeah. I got her.

It started to make sense that Janice had trained with her. From what little I had seen of both of them, it looked like their management styles really clicked. Janice was, luckily, much less abrasive than Katty, though.

"So," she said, "take a look around. I gotta pick up a few boxes of cheese from the Harwood store. Michelle is here if you have any questions. When I get back, you're going to give me a tour of my store and rate it whatever you would if you were the

141

manager on duty."

Oh, great. How was I supposed to rate a store like this? This is the fucking flagship store of the district. I couldn't give it anything less than a two, since it makes its numbers so well, but I couldn't give it two because I needed to show that I had attention to detail. Whatever I did, I needed to make sure I did it right. I didn't want Katty's wrath targeted at me, after all. I tried to think of anything I could possibly use to justify whatever I rated the store.

"Wait," I said, "do you have a copy of your score card that I can look at?"

She paused and smiled.

"I'm glad you asked," she said. "You know how to read the score card. Means know what you're doing."

She opened a drawer underneath the counter and pulled out a stack of papers, then handed them to me.

"This is your store's paperwork. Janice faxed everything over. You've got Year-to-Date and Month-to-Date in there," she said. "When I get back, rate your store to me, but give me a tour through mine."

Well, that made things easier at least. It's a good thing I asked.

She was gone a good while, but it gave me time to study the paperwork and look through the store. While she was gone, John quietly expressed a few problems to the cook. I couldn't make out what they were, but he seemed *pretty worried* about them. Every time I walked by, he'd stop talking. Instinctively, I wanted to stop and talk to him about it to see if there was anything I could do, but I knew I had a job to do. The cook, Jose, followed up nearly every one of John's whispers by loudly telling him to talk to Katty, but he never liked that answer.

While I waited, I tried to put together a spiel, which is how we're typically supposed to start a tour. The opening spiel is very · important, at least to corporate. They expect us to have one ready, not just for each store visit, but also when the closing manager walks in. They say it's important so you can quickly give your store a rating, which is apparently crucial. *What would we ever do without a rating?*

Looking at the facts, I tried to think of what I was going to rate her store. Given how clean and organized it was, it very much deserved a two, but I knew her standards were different than mine and I didn't want to look like I didn't have attention to detail. Given the score cards from my store, it deserved a four, but I didn't want to be *that guy.* You know, the hot shot who comes in and pretends he knows everything.

Before I could decide, she walked back in.

John quickly grabbed her attention. She went almost immediately to the back of the store, carrying a few thirty-pound boxes of cheese. John rushed to open the walk-in cooler door for her and propped it open after she went by.

"Is there more?" he asked.

"Nope," she said, "that's it."

He helped her put the boxes away, and stood awkwardly by her for a few moments after they finished. She gave him that look, telling him to get back to work, but he wasn't moving.

"What's wrong with you?" she asked.

"Hey," he said, "Katty."

"Hi John," she said. "What's wrong with you?"

"So..." he said, "I know that I'm scheduled off at seven today..."

"I know that as well," she said, "go on."

"Well..." he thought and paused, "my... um, my daughter is having her birthday party today... and I was wondering if I could—"

She stopped him mid-sentence, thrusting her pointer finger upward and shushing him loudly. She took a step closer to him and calmly placed her hand on his shoulder.

"Say no more," she said. "What time do you need to leave?"

John looked at her in disbelief. He clearly didn't think he'd get this far, so he had no clue what to say.

"Um..." he said, "what?"

To John's displeasure, Katty's sympathetic face almost instantly disappeared. Her eyes narrowed, her lips pulsed, and her nostrils flared. He ran out of time.

"*You deaf?*" she asked. "*What time do you need to leave?*"

"It, uh," he said, "it starts at five."

She scoffed at him.

"You gonna wear your work uniform?" she asked.

He looked down at his sauce-stained uniform and tried to brush the cheese off.

"Well," he said, "no... I guess not."

"Okay," she said and threw her hands to her hips, "what time do you need to leave?"

"I guess..." he said, "I think, maybe four?"

Katty took a moment to regain her calm. She looked around at the store and examined the progress that everyone had made so far. Her demeanor slowly faded back to the calm, yet powerful figure it was before.

"Okay!" she said and started to smile, "make sure that you get your prep done and you're out by four."

He didn't know what to do. He paused once again, propping his mouth open to say something, but closing it every few seconds. Katty looked back toward him and raised her eyebrow.

"Go!" she said.

John went.

"Alright,what are you most proud of?" Katty asked me.

Well, this was off to a bad start. I had no idea what I was most proud of. I took a quick peek at the score card and looked around the store once more.

"Cleanliness..." I stated.

"You sure?" she asked.

No. I wasn't sure. I had no idea what I was most proud of about a store that I'd never been in before. Plus, we were combining the score card of one store with the "in the moment" peek at another store. How could I possibly have picked out what I was most proud of? I felt like was given a poster of a dinosaur that was split in half, a ripped up picture of a bunch of kittens, and a roll of duct tape, then asked to write an essay on how the combined product expresses the human condition. The fact that I was able to piece together a rating and opening spiel should've been enough. The "store" that I was touring didn't even exist. It wasn't even possible! *Oh, hey Tony, what are you most proud of?*

Oh, cleanliness? That's interesting. Are you sure? Fuck you.

"Yes," I said, "I'm sure."

She smiled.

"So, the *Triple S,*" she said, "Safe, Sanitized, and..."

"...Stocked," I said, "yes, ma'am. The Triple S."

Pizza Corp loves their acronyms—okay *yeah* that's not an acronym. You know what I mean.

"So, Triple S is what you're most proud of," she said. "How did you achieve that?"

Really? Seriously. *That was* where we were going... Okay, whatever. I pulled apart my ass-cheeks and opened the flood gates.

"*Well,*" I said, "the first thing we needed to attain was the establishment of effective teams. We needed an environment where our team could collaborate on projects together and manage their tasks effectively. The best way to achieve this is the P.U.R.E. atmosphere. As you know, that's the spirit, personality, past, present, and future of Pizza Corp. It encompasses the harmony and the environment that all of our team members experience while working at the Corp."

God. I needed a shower.

P.U.R.E stands for Patron's Ultimate Restaurant Experience. It was a relatively new acronym, but the corporate office was pressing it pretty hard and was pretty adamant about getting us to say it. In all actuality, though, it had only been around for a few months. Before that, we used the saying, 'Core of the Corp,' which at least made a little more sense. I estimated that P.U.R.E. would phase out at the latest by the end of the year—at least I hoped to God it would.

"We needed to really encourage a culture that we could all appreciate, while giving our guests a fast and friendly attitude," I blabbered mindlessly. "Not only are our seasoned team members eligible to earn great benefits and tuition reimbursement, but there are many programs to help start building an effective team in our store."

Alright, before you go off wondering how healthcare benefits and paid tuition can be misleading, let me lay this out for you.

To qualify for healthcare or tuition reimbursement, you have to be considered full-time by company standards. Meaning, you have to get promoted to or hired externally for a shift manager position or higher. I once tried to take advantage of our healthcare package as a shift manager, but alas, I found out that I'd be paying two hundred dollars per month; if I were to take myself to the doctor for any notable reason, they'd be paying for virtually nothing—I'd hit my out-of-pocket before I'd hit my deductible. In turn, after a few doctors' appointments, I'd have to pay the same amount as I'd normally have to pay *without* insurance until my deductible was met. My deductible would have been twenty-five hundred dollars. Long story short: Two hundred per month, two cheap visits, and no help from insurance until I spent two and a half *thousand* dollars. I made eight dollars per hour. *Yeah, right.* Even paying the Obamacare taxes for not having insurance, I'd still be saving money.

As for tuition reimbursement, let's not kid ourselves. Sure, Pizza Corp offers a substantial program for paid tuition, but once again, in order to qualify for the program, you have to be full-time. Here's the catch: in order to be full-time, you're required to have open availability, which means Pizza Corp can schedule you whenever the hell they want. On top of that, the program demanded that you have a certain amount of on-campus hours per paid semester. If you don't attend your on-campus classes, you don't get reimbursed for your classes.

So, since Pizza Corp can schedule you whenever they want, really the tuition reimbursement program is like someone offering you a thousand-dollar prepaid visa card under the condition that you don't activate it or scratch off the security tag.

"We need associates with the drive to make a powerful difference and that starts with recognition," I said. "What better way to do that than to write out *Teamwork Tomatoes?*"

I quickly glanced over to the wall next to the phones and POS devices to verify that the employees had been writing cards for each other, and yes. They were. This store had countless cards all over the wall, from top to bottom.

Granted, we had the same amount—but they were all written by George.

The tour continued for a good few hours. John actually left before I did, which was fine by me since I had to close that night at my store anyway. It wasn't like I had the chance to go home. Katty continued to ask me questions about corporate, my store, Pizza Corp, acronyms, and lots of other things. I could tell that she was disappointed with most of my responses, but I kept hoping that I was able to talk my way out of most of the unpleasant ones. In the end, I left unconfident yet content. I did the best that I could, at least that's what I told myself. I ended up leaving at a little after five o'clock.

On the way back, though, I got a call on my cell phone. It was Max.

Driving back, I thought about how I could make the schedule work for the rest of the week. Dominic wasn't healing as fast as they had estimated from his last surgery, so Max couldn't make it to work for at least a few more days. I had some ideas, but I knew that I wouldn't be able to fix anything until I saw the schedule for myself.

I pulled up into a parking spot and sat there for a minute watching the sun sink down into the evening sky. I didn't know what I was going to tell Janice, and I knew she was going to ask. I was sure she'd have some questions about the bruises on my face, and about Max's schedule. Regardless of my worries, though, I looked at my store from the parked car, gazed at the setting sun, and somehow felt a little at home. At least, I was glad to be back at my store. As much as I bitched about it, I knew that I felt comfortable there. On some level, I belonged there. I knew the people there, I knew how to run a shift there, and as much as it pained me to admit it, I didn't want to go anywhere else... *other than home.*

I got out of the car and headed inside but as I approached the door, it slammed open and nearly hit me.

"You can't just wait a few days?" George yelled. "You can't just try to figure it out?!"

He stormed out and Janice closely followed him. I had to jump aside as they flew past me. George wasn't going on delivery, he wasn't even wearing a name-badge. He wasn't carrying a bag and didn't have anything in his hands other than his hat... and the little Batman action figure from the desk. What the *fuck* was going on?

"George, come back inside," said Janice. "Let's talk about

this!"

He sprinted to his car and stuck his arm through the open slot of the passenger-side window and turned the knob to roll it down.

"Look, Miss," said George, "here's how it works. You just said that it's *Mitch's* decision. You just said that. If it is, *you can't change it.* He's made up his mind, that's how Mitch works! He makes up his mind and does things! That's what he does! And you know what things he usually does? Usually, really stupid things!"

He tossed his stuff through the window, then opened the door, locked it, and shut it again. It took him a couple of seconds to realize what he'd done, or really what he didn't do. He tried to open it from the outside to no avail. He reached his arm into the window again to unlock the car, and gave up when he opened the door. Problem solving was never one of George's strengths. He slammed door, kicked it a few times, and stomped his foot. Janice used this time to walk around to the driver side and when George looked back up, she leaned on the door, waiting for him.

"You done?" she asked.

He kicked the tire and stared at her. Janice raised her eyebrow.

"How about now?" she asked.

He made a loud sigh, pouted, and scoffed.

"It looks like it," he said.

She scoffed and promptly asked him, "Do you need five more minutes?"

George made a sarcastic chuckle.

"No," he said and made a quiet sigh, "I'm just going to go home."

"George," said Janice, "come on. Let's talk about it. We can get through this."

I propped the driver door open and held it for him, but I knew that he wasn't going to walk through it.

"George," I said, "come on, man. What happened?"

He scoffed and walked around to the driver-side. Janice stepped aside as he got in and drove away. Janice stood still, looking down at her feet until the sound of his car completely faded. Tapping her foot impatiently, she looked back at the setting autumn sun. It was cloudy, bright, and it took up our entire view. It was like the sun buried itself into a dazzling, vivid painting that stretched infinitely into the evening sky. From behind us, the stars started to glimmer and the moon innocently peeked out to get a glimpse of the irreproachable canvas of the heavens. Janice took a deep breath and admitted that it was time to head inside.

Wait. If George was gone, who was my Spanish speaker?

"I'm going to Sonic and grabbing some coffee," Janice said. "Can I get you anything?"

I shook my head.

"What happened with George?" I asked.

"I'll tell you when I get back," she said. "How was Pre-MAPP?"

"Yeah… I'll tell you in a minute," I sighed. "Go get some coffee first."

She handed me the clipboard and headed out the driver-door. I took a look at the schedule and looked up at Juan, who had been there since eight-thirty in the morning. He was scheduled off at four. It was after six. There he was, though, doing prep for the evening rush, searching through all of the coolers, shelves, and boxes, making sure everything was ready.

"Juan," I told him, "you ever stop working?"

"Hey, man," he said, "you know me."

"How late are you staying today?" I asked.

He paused and pointed toward the clipboard. As my eyes followed his finger, he pulled the sweaty hairnet from his tattooed forehead.

"You don't have a cook tonight," he said, "Janice asked me to stay. Between you and me, if it was anyone else closing tonight, I would've said no."

I grinned and looked at him right in the eye.

"You mean…" I said, "if it was Crabby."

He grinned and we kept the silence for a few moments. He pointed and lightly tapped Janice's name on the clipboard, then went back to the make-table.

"I said anyone," he said. "I mean what I say."

Well, at least I had my Spanish speaker. I peered through the schedule again and made my own chicken-scratch version before I hopped on to help him.

"I hear you went to Pre-MAPP," he said.

I started stretching the dough to make stuffed crust, which isn't easy, mind you. It takes concentration, even for a seasoned cook. First, you have to put a wad of un-stretched dough on a pan. Then, you have to stretch it to an extra-large size without ripping it. If it rips in the middle, you can't fix it; you'd have to throw it out, since the dough is too greasy to put back together. After that, you have to put five slices of string cheese around the edges and roll the dough over it, then tuck it in. Once again, without ripping it. Once that's done, stamp the inside edges of the cheese to make sure that it doesn't fall apart in the oven. It's a pain in the ass to do during a rush, but making them when it's slow is kind of soothing, almost relaxing. It was nice to have a small break from everything else that was going on.

155

"Yeah," I said, "I went to Pre-MAPP How'd you know?"

"Doesn't matter," he said. "How'd you do?"

I prepped a few more pizzas.

"Well," I told him, "I'm... I'm not sure yet."

"You need to have some faith," he said. "You did fine."

"How do you know?" I asked.

"God told me," he said.

I stopped and stared at him. He paid me no mind and kept going for a few minutes until he looked up once again and made a shit-eating grin.

"Well?" I asked.

Juan laughed.

"Janice said so," he said. "You got a two. You got a lot of feedback, but you got a two. Looks like you get to move on to the next round."

I was relieved, but I wanted to hear it from Janice. Thinking about it in retrospect, though, I was glad that Juan was the one to tell me. If I couldn't have George there, at least I had Juan. I knew he didn't want to be there, but I really appreciated his help. Not only did I appreciate that he was working a double for me, I enjoyed his company. I didn't respect very many people, but I respected him. I hadn't had time to see a lot of my family in the last year or so, so while my wife and I were going through all of our problems, Juan was almost like family.

"I got you a cup," said Janice.

She walked back in and sat a smaller cup on the counter and opened the plastic bag that came with the drinks.

"I'm not sure how you like your coffee so I just brought you a little of everything," she said.

She placed the bag next to the cup and I had a look inside. I wasn't particularly in the mood, but I appreciated the gesture. After grabbing a few creams and artificial sweeteners and mixing them in, I had a few sips and pretended to enjoy it. It wasn't bad, but it wasn't good either, and I needed to get back to work. It was going to be a hell of a night. Plus, I desperately needed to be caught up on whatever it was that had happened to George.

Janice made a long sigh and drank her coffee.

"You ready?" she asked.

"Yes ma'am," I told her.

We sat back at the corner table. I waited for her to finish organizing her notes while I flipped through the clipboard once more. For the longest time, we sat there quietly.

She leaned forward in the chair and put her head in her hands, which was shockingly contradictory to her prompt, upbeat posture that she'd had during the manager meeting just a few days ago. Just looking at her, I could tell she was exhausted. This store was already eating her alive. She looked at her paperwork disinterestedly, almost as if she were completely detached from the situation as a whole. She looked for something to say, but resorted to saying nothing.

The few moments of eye contact we shared weren't that of work-related stress, either. It was the look of grief. She wanted company. Someone to share it with. Even if she didn't have any interest in telling me what it was, I knew that sitting with her was the least that I could do.

"What's up?" I asked.

I sipped my coffee, and pulled the notes from her hands. On the first page was a printed store visit from Mitch, outlining all of the "opportunities" that he had noticed while he was in our store. It wasn't the best report I'd ever seen. In fact, I've even seen Crabby do better than that.

"Where do I start?" she asked, clearly not talking about the paperwork.

"It doesn't matter," I said. "Just pick a spot and go."

She tapped on the table a few times, getting her mind back in running order. Thinking about what she was going to say next, she sipped her coffee, held it close for a few seconds, then dedicated herself to the task at hand.

"Mike called and quit," she said.

"Fantastic," I said. "It's alright. We can make it."

She nodded.

"I also got a call from Mitch today," she said. "You passed your Pre-MAPP You got a two."

"Awesome," I said and put on a grin like a Mr. Potato Head. "That's good, right?"

"Well," she said, "yes. It is good. But when he got the call from Katty, he took a look at our store's numbers for the week and saw Max's from a few days ago."

Great. Why wouldn't that happen? Why would we just be able to learn from our mistake and move on? But mostly, why did all of this shit have to happen at the exact *same fucking time?* Of course Mitch would pull up the scores from the first day that Max went back on the road which is coincidently the day that all hell broke loose. *Of course* that would happen right when all of this was happening with George, one of our fastest drivers. Of course all of this was happening at the same fucking time as I was in the process of being promoted.

None of this shit could wait a week? It all had to happen right now? *Seriously*—what was this, *Battlestar Galactica?!* I felt overwhelmed and completely discombobulated.

"What did he say?" I asked, although I was pretty sure I knew the answer.

"He said that if she's going to be your replacement, she's going to have to bring her driving scores up. If she doesn't, he's not going to promote her. In fact, he's going to ask me to let her go. Which means we wouldn't have a replacement, and after all this, I doubt he'd accept another one."

Yep. I was right. I knew the answer. I guess I couldn't blame him, though. He only visits this store once every few months, so he doesn't know how bad the area is. Moreover, he wasn't there the night that everything happened. For all he knew, Max was just a driver who forgot to clock back in from her delivery and started doing other things. If her scores stayed that low, she would clearly be a bad candidate for promotion.

"Now," said Janice, "I don't know why her scores were that low that day, but I do know that you were the manager on duty. I'm not going to reprimand you for what happened, and I'm not going to discipline her. Although, I feel like I should."

I nodded silently.

"All I'm going to do is ask for your partnership and trust," she said. "If there is anything that I should know about what happened that night, I'm trusting you to tell me."

Max would've killed me if I told Janice, I just knew it. I only had two choices and since I didn't know what to do, I decided to go with the wrong one.

"Is there anything that I need to know about?" she asked.

I shook my head.

"Nope. Whatever it is, I'll fix it," I said, with no idea how.

"Good," she said. "Lastly, Mitch is already interviewing assistant manager positions for this store, so I bumped your MAPP up to Wednesday. That's the closest one. I'll be working with Max, getting her ready for her MAPP by Monday."

"Wow. That's... that's really fast," I said.

"Yeah. It is, but don't stress it. I switched the management schedule around. You're off this weekend so you can take some time to rest before you go," she said. "Besides, MAPP isn't one of my biggest concerns right now."

"I'm guessing George is?" I asked.

"Well," she said, and paused for a moment. "I'm sure that will be sorted out soon. At least, I hope it will."

"What happened?" I asked.

She sighed.

"You know that George is an immigrant, right?" she asked.

"No," I said, "I didn't know that."

"Well, he is," she said. "When I got to this store, I took a leap of faith and processed everyone's background checks again. You know this already, you signed for it. George's background check got flagged, though. They're having trouble verifying his work visa."

"How long is that going to take to fix?" I asked.

"It depends on when they get back to us," she said. "Company policy is to voluntarily terminate an employee if it's

161

not verified in two weeks. We can't let them work at all until everything goes through, though, even if it looks like it will work out in the end."

"I see."

"Yeah," she said. "Tricky part is, if we let him go, he only has so long before his green card is revoked because he's not employed. So, it has the potential to snowball fast. Eventually, he might be deported."

"What can we do about it?" I asked.

"Leave it to me," she said. "Trust me. I'll take care of it. It's my mess. I'm going to clean it up."

She looked out the window at the starry sky and stood up. Picking up the papers, she knocked them on the table in a stack, put them on the clipboard, and gave the clipboard to me.

"Is there anything I can help you with to get you through tonight?" she asked.

I shook my head.

"I think you're good," I said. "Go home and get some rest."

I walked her to the door, and watched her drive off.

The night went by quickly. Although it was game night, it never got overbearingly busy. Before the rush kicked in gear,

Reece jumped in from one of his deliveries with his guitar and started to sing, but I stopped him. George wasn't there. After I told him what had happened, Reece didn't exactly feel like it either.

During the shift, I gave Max a call and asked if it was possible to come in for her shift the following day. I could hear Dominic crying in the background, but Max eventually figured out a way to make it happen. I hated that I had to ask her to do that. She needed to stay at home with Dominic so that he could recover from his surgery, but desperate times... you know.

The most difficult part about wrapping up the night was throwing away all of the pizzas that Juan prepped. There were so many, which was a good and a bad thing. The good thing was it meant that we didn't have to deal with an outrageous rush, but the bad was that I was sure that the night's slowness would destroy our labor cost percentages.

At the end of the night, I set the alarm and walked out. When I closed the door behind me, I saw a familiar face. Sitting on the cement, just around the corner, was George. With a blank stare toward the distant stars, his arms wrapped around his legs, he rested his head against the sharp bricks of the building. His batman action figure leaned on a fresh bag of gummy worms, which leaned on his backpack, which leaned loosely on the side of his hip. He, of course, leaned on Pizza Corp. It all seemed lopsided and unstable, like a small gust of wind could have knocked the whole thing down. This wasn't the George I knew.

After I locked the door behind me, I checked my phone and made sure that I had time to talk, then I quickly walked around him and sat down. I plunged my hand into the bag of gummy worms without waiting for his permission and shoveled the lot of them into my mouth.

I waited a few seconds for him to respond, but he didn't.

"Hey man," I said.

Still nothing.

"George," I said.

He took a breath and let out a long sigh. Careful not to knock anything over, he pushed one hand into the bag and grabbed Batman with the other.

"Hey, BossMan," he said. "You want some gummy worms?"

I gave him a perplexed stare.

My mouth was still full. In fact, it was work making sure that none of them fell out every time I said anything.

"No thanks," I said, barely making out the words.

"Why don't you ever take any?" said George. "I'm starting to think that you don't like gummy worms. But, then again, you have to like gummy worms. If you didn't, you wouldn't be a real person."

"George," I said, "I already had some. I took a handful when

I sat down."

He shrugged in disbelief.

"You want me to show them you?" I asked.

He made a grin, which was clearly fake.

"You want to know something?" he asked.

I nodded.

"When I first got to the U.S., I was six years old," he said. "It's funny. In my mind, I thought that everyone who lived here came from somewhere else. Even if they spoke English, I figured, maybe they grew up someplace else. It never really clicked that people were *born* here until I was way older."

I didn't say anything.

"It didn't make any sense that anyone could be born here. They had to *earn it*. It was like heaven, a kind of place that you either had to work really hard for, or something really bad had to happen to you before you could go," he said. "When I first got here, I spent weeks dreaming about the people that I met in Mexico who tried to cross the border with me. People I'll never see again. I used to have nightmares about the people I met on the way here, the people who died, the people who made it, and the people who I'm sure wished they hadn't."

I paused and looked at him.

"What was it like?" I asked.

"In Mexico?" he asked, "or crossing the border?"

"Both," I said. "Why did you have to go through all of that? Why didn't you just stay there?"

He shrugged.

"I mean that in the best possible way," I said.

He grinned and continued.

"My mom never actually told me what was going on, until everything happened," he said, "but now that I'm older, I know. It's amazing what you don't understand when you're looking through a kid's eyes."

"What do you mean?" I asked.

"When I was little, my dad would send me out door to door by myself, asking for money. I did that almost every day. He made me walk miles and miles, from house to house, by myself. I was barefoot. I had shoes, but he never let me wear them. I didn't really understand it then, but... I was making drug runs. I was taking the drugs with me in bags and the more miserable and poor I looked, the more money they would give me. My dad didn't want to go because it was dangerous and I guess because he wouldn't get as much money as I did... In a way, it was smart. Who'd shoot a little kid, right?"

I didn't say anything. I couldn't say anything. The whole concept astonished me.

"He'd send my older brother, too. We went on different routes, though. We wouldn't see each other until after dark, when we got home. Sometimes my brother wouldn't get home until way later… sometimes not even until the next morning. Dad wanted to send my sister too, but my mom wouldn't let him. One day he tried to take her anyway. She was a lot younger than me, just barely talking. My dad wanted her to go with my older brother, I guess so he could ask for more money… I don't know. But my mom tried to stop him. My mom picked her up and held her away from him. Dad was *mad*… he yelled, cursed, screamed… it was worse than I'd ever seen him. He picked up a knife and threatened her with it. That was common, though. He did *that* all the time.

"But this time, when she didn't do what he said, he grabbed his gun. He said that she needed to let my sister go, but my mom wouldn't. My brother was crying, screaming at him to stop, but he wouldn't let up. My brother kept telling him that he could get as much money as Dad wanted by himself, he said he'd stay out until he got it, but dad didn't listen. He pulled Sarah from my mom's arms, which took a long time. After he got her and started walking to the door, my sister cried on his shoulder wanting down, wanting mom… I didn't know what to do. I didn't want my brother to take Sarah, but I was scared of my dad."

"What happened?" I asked.

"When he opened the door, my mom just ran at him. She didn't care about what happened to her." he said. "My dad

167

pointed the gun at her, but my brother jumped in and tried to take it... when it went off."

George looked me in the eye, but I didn't have the nerve to look back. My eyes looked straight down toward the cement and discarded gummy worms.

"My mom fell to her knees and tried to see if he was okay... but he wouldn't move," He said. "He was just lying there, on the ground. My dad took off. We waited around for a while... I held my sister while my mom tried to wake my brother up, but he just... well, he didn't wake up."

I couldn't imagine what that would be like. I didn't want to think about it, and I didn't know what to say. I looked over to George, who was still just sitting there. He didn't move. He just stared out into the distance.

"We went to a guy's house that my mom said she knew for a long time," he said. "She told me that he knew a guy who was a Coyote and could take us to America. When she told me that, I thought that was *so* cool. It was like a fantasy story, like werewolves or something. But it wasn't anything like that."

I nodded silently, urging him to continue.

"She called him Uncle Alejandro," he said. "Looking back, I don't think he and my mom were actually related. We spent a few nights there before we left with the Coyotes, who it turned out were just normal people. Most of them weren't very nice.

Actually, they were pretty much all assholes."

"That's when you crossed the border..." I said.

"No, not quite," he said, "but almost. You know that wall that Donald Trump always said that he wants to build?"

"Yeah," I said.

"Well," he said, "there's already one like it. But you don't go over it... you go under it. Through caves, like the ones in San Antonio. Only you need a Coyote to guide you or else you'll get lost... and never find your way out."

"Caves," I said, nodding. "You don't go through the river?"

"Oh, hell no," said George. "I mean, you can try. But the Coyotes always told us that the people who try to cross the river either get shot or drown."

George sighed.

"I guess they might not... I believed them when I was a kid, but I don't know... Anyway, every night, the Coyotes split us into different areas. One for boys, and one for girls," he said. "I always hated that... I could hear the girls screaming on the other side, even though it was far away. I didn't want to think about what it was they were screaming about. I always stayed up and listened for my mom's voice, or my sister, but luckily I never heard either of them. It was always someone else, but it was always someone different every night. Sometimes it was a lot of people."

"The day that we went in through the caves, they gave us a

gallon of water each and told us that what we had was all that we were going to get until we were on the other side. Me and my sister had to share one. I remember looking at it and thinking that it was a lot. I didn't think that I'd have to worry about it, but we stayed in the caves for what felt like days... and by the time we got out, my water was gone. Once, while my mom was sleeping, some other guy came up and tried to steal it, because I guess he ran out. I wouldn't let him have it, not because it was mine, but because I knew I had to share it with my sister, but he pushed me down and took it. Luckily another member of our group saw it and started a fight with him. It woke a lot of people up. By the end of it, they got the water back from him and they told him to go away... and sent him out on his own. I remember all of us moving on after that... and hearing his voice for the next few days. At the beginning, he was just yelling and cursing, but after a while he started shrieking and wailing nonsensical things, like he was going crazy. One day, we woke up, and the screaming stopped. We could hear him moaning, and saying things every few hours, but after that, we didn't hear him anymore."

"I can't imagine," I told him.

"Well, it didn't mean much as a kid," George said, "but, now that I'm older, it's hard to think about... I mean, that guy's dead now. *He died.* I... still can't quite wrap my mind around it."

I grabbed a gummy worm and stuck it in my mouth, then I

offered another one to him. He turned it down.

"I don't know," he said, "I tried to do everything right. When first got here, my mom told me that it was going to be hard, so she started us on the right path to be citizens. She enrolled me in school, and after a while, she enrolled my sister. I learned how to speak English, I did all the paperwork to work legally, and during high school, I took ROTC. It sounds cheesy, but one of the first things I saw when I got here was a poster of Uncle Sam, and I thought that was *so fucking cool.* I saw all of these other kids who's parents were in the military and I really wanted to be a part of that. I wanted to be like them. I wanted to be a *war hero* who had kids that were *born* here. Fuck yeah, right? How much more badass can you get?!"

I nodded.

"The Marines said that they'll take care of my citizenship once I join." he said. "If I play my cards right, that's what I want to do."

"What do you have to do?" I asked. "It sounds like you're almost there."

He sighed.

"I've gotta get my residency if I want to join the Marines. I've already got my paperwork put in, but I need to go back to Mexico to get proof that I'm a citizen there. That's the last thing I have to do," he said. "But I have to take my family with me...

and I don't want to do that. They said they might be able to get it done without me getting proof of citizenship, but I'd have to pay a little over a thousand dollars. I'm okay with that, I just have to save up the money."

"I see," I said.

In that moment, I hoped Janice was serious about making sure George still had this job. George had come this far and I couldn't bear to see him stop now. I just had one question. There was one thing that didn't quite make sense to me.

"George," I said, "can I ask a question?"

"Go for it, BossMan," he said.

"How did you start driving?" I asked. "Without citizenship, do you have a driver's license?"

George sighed.

"Nope. I don't," he said. "Remember when I started, how I was just a CSR?"

I nodded.

"Well, we started running pretty short on drivers, so after a few months, Crabby bumped me up," he said. "She didn't check to see if I had a license, and she didn't run a background or anything, so I didn't question it."

I sighed.

"You know," I said, "That's probably why Janice had an issue when she processed your background check. If she processed it as a driver, you probably came up—"

"—Yeah," said George. "I know."

"You think we can trust her to get everything taken care of?" I asked.

He nodded.

"She's strict," he said, "but she's not mean."

I sighed and started to get up. George did as well. As he pulled himself upward, his backpack let loose and the bag of gummy worms fell. Before he realized it, there were worms all over the cement around his feet.

"Just like you always say," said George, "everyone goes through weird shit sometimes. You have your wife, Juan has his past, Max has Dominic and her husband… everyone has something."

"Yeah," I said. "No one works at Pizza Corp because they want to."

George nodded. He picked up one of the worms, blew off some of the dirt, and put it in his mouth.

"Nobody," he said. "Not a single one of us."

CHAPTER 5

That feel when you get to work and it's not on fire.

After two days off consecutively, it was always difficult dealing with customers again. Not just because I was numb and really just didn't care about them, but because they always had something completely ridiculous to complain about.

Don't get me wrong, there are people who have a right to complain—George might be deported, Max is a single mom trying to raise a kid who needs spinal surgery, my wife has cancer, and the list goes on... but customers are always quick to remind me how selfish they are, right from the moment they open their stupid mouths.

"What, you don't have any bags?!" she asked Janice. "So... I'm just going to have to carry it out with my hands?!"

After examining the place for a bit and confirming my preset expectation that the store was a massive dump, I walked past Janice and tried to stay quiet so that I didn't get dragged in that "Customer Experience" issue. I thought about listening in, but decided that it was a better idea to start setting up for my shift that night. In the back of the store, I noticed the clipboard on the desk and pulled it off. I paced toward the front of the store again. Janice noticed me and we had a small, unspoken greeting with our eyebrows.

Juan was on the schedule again, that poor guy. At least he was getting his hours. Knowing Janice, I assumed that he got paid for all of them. My drivers were Reece and Max. Max had MAPP that day, too. She was pulling a double.

I looked further down on the schedule and saw Crabby. She was scheduled for a mid-shift but she still wasn't there.

I shrugged it off and went on my way.

After a few moments, the driver door opened and Max's voice echoed from outside of it. It squeaked open a little more, allowing Reece to race inside. Haphazardly throwing his delivery bag on the rack, he darted past Max toward the driver computer and checked back in from his delivery.

Reece was quick. Just after he checked in, he grabbed the next delivery bag and went on his way. Max held the door open for him and then slowly walked in. There was something weird about her, though. She was... wait. Was she wearing lipstick?

She was.

And slacks, and a *decently revealing* button-down shirt.

Holy shit.

She walked up to the driver's POS and clocked in for the day. When she turned around to greet me, though, I had to be sarcastic.

"Well, well, well," I told her. "Aren't you all dressed up?"

Her right eyebrow rocketed into the sky like Apollo 11.

"You can shut your whore mouth, Tony," she said, pointed to her eye-liner, and scrolled with her finger down her outfit. "I had MAPP today. Don't expect *all this* to be a normal thing."

"I wouldn't mind seeing it again," I said, taking a step back from the sarcasm. "You look nice. How did you do?"

She shrugged. Looking down at her outfit, it was like she was quietly second guessing herself. She took a moment to button up her shirt a bit more as she thought about what to say, and in that quick moment, I hated myself.

"I'm not sure," she said and started to pick at the rest of her clothes. "I didn't overdo it, did I?"

"Max," I said and looked into her eyes, "you look great."

She looked to the floor and back at me.

"How did you do?" I asked.

She thought for a second and started to talk, but she was interrupted by the "Ring for Service" bell.

It was Janice's customer. She was still there.

"*It says RING BELL FOR SERVICE!*" she said and continued to ring the bell. "When a customer rings this bell, don't you think she should get service?"

"I'm sorry, ma'am," said Janice, who had seriously just turned around. "Your service is our priority. We're shorthanded and I was about to make an order for another cust—"

"Whatever, bitch!" she shouted. "This is the worst restaurant experience I've ever had!"

With that, she started marching off. She stomped and flailed around so much I was surprised that she didn't drop her pizzas. After a few moments, she reached the door and pulled it open.

"And what kind of establishment doesn't *give their customers bags*?! That's standard customer service!" she shouted.

I looked on the driver's utility drawer next to me and couldn't resist—I knew I'd get scolded by Janice for what I was about to do, but I didn't care. I pulled out the drawer and grabbed some small, pocket sized plastic silverware bags. They were covered with dust, so I shook the top one off and rubbed the dust on my slacks.

"Ma'am, I'm sorry for the inconvenience but I found some!" I told her.

Janice's reaction was priceless. She looked at me as if I'd found the missing link, then looked at the bag like a raisin she found in her chocolate chip muffin.

I walked toward the door, trying desperately to hide its size. She stood with the door open and held the box out toward me and when I walked up, I unfolded the bag and just put it on top of the box.

"You wanted a bag for your cutlery, right?" I said and chuckled pseudo-nervously. "I'm assuming so, anyway. There's not really a reason to bag a pizza box."

We stared in each other's eyes for several seconds while everyone around us stopped talking—the restaurant was dead quiet… and then the wind, I'm not shitting you, just blew the bag away.

There was a priceless pause as all of us, employees and customers, watched the bag float merrily in the wind down the sidewalk and into the street.

"I'm sorry about that, ma'am," I said, trying my damnedest to keep from smiling. "Would you like another bag?"

She shook her head.

"Okay, ma'am." I said and gave her a shit-eating grin. "I hope you have a Pizza Corp day!"

No, I have no fucking clue what that was supposed to mean.

As I walked back behind the counter, she let out a loud growl, slammed the door behind her and marched off.

It's the little things in life you treasure.

"Okay," Janice said, "now that both of you are here, we need to talk."

She sat me and Max down at the table, which seemed to have started to become her manager meeting table. She looked us square in the face.

"Mitch had a visit today on his way to MAPP," she said. "During that visit, he said that on one of the days last week, the alarm wasn't set until after two a.m. and when he looked at your numbers, he noticed that you didn't check back in from your delivery until almost midnight. He also received countless emails and phone calls regarding customer complaints from that day. I'm giving you *one chance* to tell me what the *hell* is going on."

Max and I looked at each other and back at her. Neither of us knew what to say. Should we tell her? I couldn't tell her without Max's approval, but it was looking like I wouldn't have the choice.

Minutes passed, still nothing.

Janice plopped the M.O.D. clipboard on the table and pressed it with the palm of her hand with so much force that it started wrinkling the paper.

"Look," she said and pushed it off the edge. It splattered on the floor and paper went everywhere. She didn't even budge.

"I don't care about protocol. I don't care about what rules you've broken, and I don't care how many. I just want to know what happened last week, and I want you to be honest. If I'm going to support you and vouch for you, you've got to be honest with me. I need to be in the loop. If you don't tell me what the hell happened that night, I'm going to have to pull you from this whole thing and let you both go," she said. "Trust me, I don't want to do that. Not just because I like both of you, but because we're really shorthanded and really need the help. But I will, and damn the consequences."

Max looked toward me and nodded.

It didn't take but a second. Right then and there, we spilled the whole platter of beans. We told her everything. And I have to say, it made me feel a little better.

There was a long silence. It felt uncomfortable, but the look on Janice's face settled the mood a bit. At least she wasn't angry.

"I..." Max started and took a moment to make sure she had permission to talk.

"I have no intention of letting this get in the way. At least, as far as I can help it," she said. "I'm scheduled to drive tonight. I'll be driving."

Janice's eyes became bloodshot. She tried to hold her anger back but couldn't any more. With a loud thud, she slammed her fist onto the table and jolted up. The table creaked with her weight and struggled to hold it. Janice's energy pulsed at us like Iron Man taking down an entire enemy fleet with a single blow.

"*No. You. Will. Not,*" said Janice. "We're going to do this the right way or not at all."

We conversed and formed a plan for what felt like hours. Janice was going to tell Mitch about the accident. It was too late to write up an accident report, but we could make sure that she wouldn't drive. To cover all of Mitch's time-consuming corporate babble, Janice told us that she was going to assure him that she'd talk to us about the proper way to handle that kind of situation and then assured *us* that she'd sit us down and make damn sure we understood. After the talk, we got up and started to go over the visit.

She took us back behind the counter and showed us around, giving us the tour. Since our store had two employees that were being MAPP'ed, Mitch undoubtedly had a fair amount to say about it. The first stop was by the registers, which we promptly noticed were fully detailed and dust-free.

"Alright," said Janice, "so, for starters, he gave us a three. So, that's good."

She handed the clipboard over to me.

"We need to work on our cleanliness, he rated us a four on that," she said. She was obviously very, very tired and ready to quickly get this over with and go home. "He also gave us a four on Recognition. The only saving grace he gave us was a two on efficiency and on our P.U.R.E Product."

That could only mean one thing. Some of our employees were filling out surveys—I mean, *it couldn't have been our customers.* It was probably George. That was a common theme with him. We wouldn't know what his comments were for another few weeks, though. Even after we got those in, though, we still wouldn't have a name. If it was George, though, we'd know. I was willing to bet that at least one of those surveys included a comment about Janice saving the company from hobgoblins or something.

"Let's go look at the board," Janice said.

We walked over to the Teamwork Tomatoes board, where Max and I immediately noticed the changes from the day before. Everything was empty. All of the old Teamwork Tomatoes were cleared out.

"Mitch decided that we needed to draw for our Team Member of the Month," said Janice.

As we discussed earlier, the Team Member of the Month Program was Pizza Corp's way of rewarding its employees. The process was simple. Each month, the store manager was supposed to remove all of that month's Teamwork Tomatoes and put them in a bucket, then draw one at random. The employee whose name was on the card was then considered Team Member of the Month and received an extra twenty dollars on their next paycheck.

Now, here's the thing. Each month when a Teamwork Tomato is drawn, not only is it put up on the wall for everyone to see, it's also sent via email to our district manger, every single store in our district, *and* our regional manager. The regional manager then forwards all of the winning Teamwork Tomatoes to our region's media department so that they can put all of them into that month's Core of the Corp employee magazine. Luckily, since there are so many emails going around during the first of the month, it's pretty easy to hide under the radar if your store forgets or *neglects* to draw a Teamwork Tomato. So, in the past, no one has paid any attention to our lack of employees of the month. This month, however, Mitch was giving us a tour. Since he conducted the tour on the first day of the month, he was required to report the winner of the draw, which meant Lindsay was expecting an email from him containing the winning Teamwork Tomato.

In turn, the first Team Member of the Month from our location *in seven months* was emailed throughout the company... and there was no hiding from it.

The *winning Teamwork Tomato for the month of November...* *sigh* ... *looked like this:*

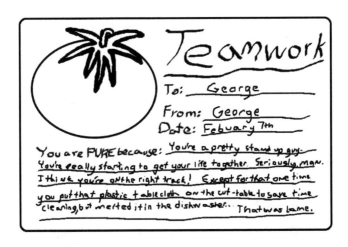

So, yeah. That happened.

Since George was considered terminated, I wonder how they were planning on giving him his extra twenty dollars.

A good while passed after Janice left. We had a few customers and a small rush but nothing compared to what I figured we'd have. It was almost frightening.

We cleaned as we went, and by the time we closed our doors the place was clean. Throughout the night, since Juan didn't have a car and we kept Max inside, Reece was the only driver out taking deliveries. He didn't care. At first he was flustered, but as the tips started coming in, he stopped giving a shit. I got permission from Janice to raise the delivery time to an hour. She said that she'd take it up with Mitch if he bothered to ask about it. We eventually sent Juan home. For a while it was just Max and me. I'd be lying if I said it wasn't relaxing.

"Plastic, floppy things are weird," said Max.

Wh-what?

"I mean, like," she said, "not dildo things."

She bopped a plastic whisk in her hand from side to side. It was a standard red colored Pizza Corp whisk that, in that familiar Pizza Corp fashion, was admirably terrible at doing its job of whisking things.

I just kind of stared at her for a second and chuckled.

She laughed aloud.

Together, we made a good sigh. It was nice.

"So... how did MAPP go?" I asked.

She sighed and looked at the whisk. She lifted her eyebrow, and put the whisk back up.

"It... uh," she said, "it went."

I dumped out my dust pan and moved closer to her. After putting a few more dishes up, she looked into the sink and started to wash her hands. She stepped away from the dishwasher and tripped over herself a bit, looking for something to do or say.

"Almost done on this end," she said.

"Awesome," I told her. "Just a few more things and we'll be good to go."

"Good to go," she said with a slight stutter, "We'll make like banana and split."

I nodded.

"We'll make like a rectum," she said, "and get the crap out of here."

Dammit.

"Make like a baby..." I said, "... and head out."

She raised an eyebrow.

"We'll make like a prom dress," she said, "and take off."

187

I chuckled and walked over to put the broom up behind her and we both started taking bags out of the garbage cans.

"So..." I said, "it was that bad?"

Max sighed.

"What happened?" I asked.

Fiddling with the next bag, she bit her bottom lip. She started to say something, but after muttering the first part of a word, she stopped again. After a few moments, she resorted to just looking into the infinity of thoughts that currently rested in a dirty, used Personal Pizza Box on top of a bunch of garbage in the trash can.

"Nothing happened, exactly..." she started, "I... I don't know."

"Max," I told her, "don't worry. I'm sure you did fine."

I thought about taking the bag out of the garbage can that she was staring into, but decided not to. I didn't want to distract her.

"Even if it didn't turn out as well as we wanted, we'll push through," I said. "We're in this together. I've got you."

She sighed.

"Nothing bad happened," she said.

"Then... what's wrong?"

She shrugged.

"Crabby was there," she said.

"What?" I asked. "Why?"

"I don't know. She was talking to Mitch while I interviewed

with Katty," she said. "I think that part went okay, but I don't know what Crabby was doing there."

She started working on the next trash can.

"I don't know, Tony. I'm sure it was about that night last week. He probably asked her for her opinion of me... and you know that she and I don't *exactly get along...* "

She stared back down into the canister.

"I... I think I messed everything up," she said. "I'm sorry.... This is my fault."

Crabby might have been the person to tell Mitch that the alarm wasn't set. She probably went up there during the MAPP so she could tell him before the store visit without Janice knowing.

"Max," I told her, "I chose you for a reason. We'll get through this together."

"But Tony," she said, "I might have just lost you your promotion. *And maybe your job.*"

I paused.

"... No. It wasn't you." I told her. "You didn't do anything wrong. It was my decision to send you out there. And neither of us could've predicted what happened. Besides, if this doesn't work out, we'll try again. And we'll try again after that. Then we'll keep trying until we make it work."

She turned around and bit her lip so hard that it might have burst open. She faced the wall in front of her and tried to keep her eyes dry.

"Why me?" she asked.

"What?"

"*Why*," she said, "*Me?* We've worked together for two years and you've never put me in for a promotion. You're always there to help me when I need a day off for Dominic, and I'm grateful for that, but what's all this special attention about?"

I had to think for a second.

"Because," I said, "you're a hard—"

"No!" she said. "No. That's not it. I haven't ever done anything for you. I come in *sometimes* because I need the money but I've never done anything special. I'm not a *good* employee. I just come in, do my job, then I go home. If you think about it, I'm never here anyway. I always need to take days off and I never give you any notice. Why would you risk everything, your promotion, your career, your family, all for me? All I've ever done is let you down and make things worse!"

She turned around and threw her blue eyes into mine like a spear.

"Why are you doing this? Do you feel sorry for me? Do you think I'm *incapable* of doing it myself?! Do you think I'm a *whore* and just want to *sleep with me*?!"

She took another moment. Her eyes pressed further into

mine. I could see her heart beating out of her chest.

"I've..." she said, trying to tame her broken breath like a trainer on a bronco, "I've been down this road, you know. And I—"

She choked.

"I... I might have made mistakes before, but have standards now. That's the whole reason why I left," she said, "and if that's what you're looking for... I'm not your girl."

She put her hand on her forehead, trying desperately to repress what she felt. Her fingers soaked in her tears as she held them tightly over her eyes and forehead. She hurried backwards until her back slammed against the wall, then slid down toward the floor.

I didn't know where to start.

"And now, even if you do want to help me..." she cried, "I just ruined everything."

Just standing there, I listened to the silence. She didn't make a sound, not even a whimper. She was just on the floor with her hands on her drenched face, cuddling herself inside of her legs, sitting perfectly still... just trying to pick up the pieces.

I pulled myself to my knees and crawled next to her. After a small eternity, she turned back toward me with a stare that read like the first page of a blank notebook.

"Max," I said, trying my damnedest to smile.

Wiping her tears as best as she could, she shrugged and dragged the back of her hand across her face.

She sighed.

Becoming the self-image of a stone pillar, I leaned my head against the wall and straightened my back.

"I've said it before and I'll say it again," I told her. "We're a team. We might make mistakes, and we might fall every once in a while... but no matter what, I've got you."

I scooted myself closer to her... but still tried to give her enough space. Given the tornado that was going through her mind, I figured we didn't need any more ambiguity.

I tried to think of what to say... in situations like this, Max always said something funny—something sarcastic and stupid.

"You know I'm married, right?" I asked and instantly regretted it.

She made a soft sigh.

"Yeah, well..." she said, hiding a shattered part of herself that no one was ever meant to see. "So was I."

It was, finally, ten thirty. Thirty more minutes before we closed and the store was *done. Hell yeah.* After Reece came back, we'd be able to leave, assuming nothing terrible happened. I was cautiously optimistic. We were in the middle of the asshole zone, which is the time period between closing time and whenever the store is finished being cleaned—just the time that if a customer called and ordered something, we'd have to pull everything back out and start all over. It didn't seem likely that night, thankfully. The last hour was pretty dull, consisting of a delivery every hour or so at just the right obnoxious interval to keep Reece out of the store.

A few minutes passed and Max and I just kind of sat there on the counter, looking toward the lobby. Our feet dangled down the wooden ad for Pizza Corp's *Ten Dollar Pizza Deal* and we silently stared into the infinity of our thoughts and fears. I wished so much that I could join her, even though she was right next to me.

After a few seconds, I broke the silence.

"So..." I said, "are you still... uh... planning on doing the overnight tomorrow?"

She nodded.

"We always do," she said and started to stutter, "unless... you have someone else in mind."

"No, no," I said, trying not to show how much I felt about it, "no... I'm just making sure."

"Yep," she said, still staring into the nothingness of the burnt orange tile. She made a soft, relieved smile.

I opened my mouth to say something but was interrupted by the ring of the phone. I looked at the time on my phone. Ten forty-seven. Fuckers.

"*Of course,*" said Max, hopping off the counter.

"I got it," I said and grabbed the phone on the counter beside me.

"Thanks for calling Pizza Corp," I said, "Are you calling about a previous order or would you like to schedule a future order?"

That usually got through to most non-assholes who simply didn't realize that we were about to close.

"*Yeah, I need a million pizzas. All double pepperoni. Medium Stuffed-Crust Thin and Crispy Hand-stretched Pan. What's the difference between that and the pasta? Actually, give me both. I need extra lard to shove into my face-hole.*"

George.

"Oh yeah, I'll get right on that," I said. "What's up?"

"Hey BossMan," he said, "is, uh, is Janice there?"

I shook my head although he obviously couldn't see it. Why would he be calling so close to close if he wanted to talk to Janice?

"Nope. Sorry, man," I told him. "Why?"

He sighed in that overdramatic way that only George can.

"She gave me a huge list of stuff that I had to do by the end of today," he said. "I just wanted to let her know that I did all of the things. I figured that since she told me to finish everything by tonight that she'd be there. Maybe she'd have a better plan than just waiting, which is what she told me to do after I got all of this stuff done."

I sighed.

"I'm afraid not. Sorry, broskie," I told him. "I'm closing tonight. I'd offer to help, but I don't have a clue what's going on. She's been keeping me out of it."

"Oh," he said. "When does she work next?"

"Um…" I said and scooted over to the wall and peered at the manager schedule. "She closes tomorrow."

"Dang. I was hoping that she'd open," he said.

The schedule was all sorts of messed up. There were marks, edits, and re-writes everywhere. After a good few seconds of squinting I was able to make out the next day's schedule.

"Oh wait," I said, "she does."

I looked again, just to make sure.

"She closes, too," I said.

Damn. I guess it wasn't surprising. She's salaried and all. It just sucked that she had to be there for that long. I wondered why she chose to do it that way.

"That's crazy," said George, "but our Boss Lady is bat-shit."

"Yeah," I said.

We both hung up after a few more words. It took a second to process everything—Max, Dominic, George, MAPP, and Trinity. I took a small moment, just a small one, to wish that I had someone to talk to about the whole thing. Just to vent and ask for advice. Just someone to sit with and talk.

I eventually came to the realization that, just like George, my life had become a waiting game. There wasn't much I could do on my end other than try my best and have faith that the system would take care of everything. Unfortunately the system, especially our healthcare system, immigration system, and Pizza Corp, tends to be a heaping pile of shit.

After only about twenty more minutes, we were able to make like a tree and get the fuck out of there. I went right to bed and six hours later, I was up and ready for MAPP.

CHAPTER 6

Pizza Corp complains incessantly about the lack of options when it comes to promoting within. The problem stems from the fact that *firstly,* an employee must typically be full-time to be promoted unless their employee review is no less than miraculous; *secondly,* full-time employees are required to be offered health insurance by law; and *thirdly,* Pizza Corp—to avoid paying for health insurance—limits its full-time entry-level staff to only one or two per store, if any. Thus, there are simply not enough full-time employees to promote to shift manager positions—in turn, not enough shift managers. This leads to salaried store managers picking up the slack. Now, since *firstly*, employee satisfaction surveys are limited to hourly employees and any complaints, low ratings, or otherwise negative comments were meant to be associated with store managers and *secondly*, store managers don't have the option to fill out employee satisfaction surveys about their superiors, Pizza Corp on a district level was more or less *entirely* pleased with this problem. The complaints from district managers about the lack of available personnel to fill shift manager positions are all pretense, a façade to encourage the area and region managers to believe that they're doing their absolute best.

The only consequences are as follows:

1. Store managers are without exception unhappy and utterly dissatisfied with their lives as a whole.
2. Districts save a bunch of labor dollars that they'd otherwise be spending on shift managers.
3. *Oh no, we don't have enough shift managers, it's just so sad.*

After a few years since the passing of Obamacare, Pizza Corp finally came up with a solution to the problem. *No, not pay for health insurance, don't be silly*—each district unanimously decided to hire externally instead of promoting from within. This solved a great number of problems.

The list is as follows:
1. Stores pay less for healthcare benefits.
2. Since they have no record of employee reviews for their external hires, each interview represented a perfect candidate.
3. *No more MAPPs! Woo!*

Eventually, of course, they realized that they couldn't eliminate MAPP completely. Employees would still need the *option* of being promoted, even if it was immensely inconvenient to promote within. Their solution to that problem was to redesign the MAPP program. Instead of conducting a series of one-on-one interviews, followed by an assessment of knowledge, followed by a one-on-one floor walk with a district manager, followed by a last and final interview negotiating pay and location, the brand-spanking-new MAPP consisted of a group interview, a group floor walk, and... that's it, you're done. *Yay efficiency!*

It's amazing how little work you can spend on promoting employees when you actively avoid doing it.

Long story short, I knew what I was getting into when I pulled into the parking space. I'd never attended one of the new, lazy MAPPs, but I had a feeling that no matter how well I did, there was a solid chance that I'd get outmatched by a shiny, flawless external hire. I was going to give it my all, but considering, you know, *everything*, it wasn't likely. There was little to no way *into* the shift supervisor position and there was certainly no way out of it, but I needed to try. I walked up to the corporate office, went up the elevator and found my way to the designated MAPP area, shook hands with Mitch—who gave me one of those "Hello, My Name is" stickers—then headed into the conference room and set down at the large, rectangular table.

As I sat at the table with the other shift supervisors, one from each district, I eyed Mitch, who stood with a few other district managers at the front of the room. I didn't know the names of them, but their similar pseudo-positive attitude was familiar.

As they looked at each other and talked amongst themselves and to the group, they shared one common expression that completely contrasted their self-assurance: they all had the same dumbfounded look of confusion on their face and that same outlandish smile. They'd occasionally bring Lindsay and the other district managers up in the conversation, ask each other where she was, *where the others were*, and were they sure that they were meeting at the proper place and time—but the conversation was quickly halted after only about two or three statements on the topic. It was as if they all suspected that someone had made a grave mistake and they all quietly hoped that they weren't the one at fault for it.

Every once in a while, Mitch would come up and put his hand on my shoulder. He'd ask me about my day, how my weekend off was, how my store was improving, and so on. He'd try to make me feel more comfortable, and I respected that. He was, after all, the only person in the room who I'd met before, but the problem was that we didn't really have much to say to each other. I'd only briefly met him in passing. I'd given him a few tours of my store over the last few years, sure, but it wasn't like we knew each other on a personal level. Of course, I returned his sentiment with my own outlandish smile and corporate vomit.

After a while, a small group of store managers walked into the room, followed by the shift managers from their district. Katty walked in, too, as well as several other store managers from other districts—presumably to represent the candidates who Pre-MAPP'ed with them. At that moment, I couldn't tell whether I was relieved or worried.

When she sat down next to me, Katty leaned her eyes toward the district managers who were talking with the other store managers and just let all the muscles in her face drop, which resulted in the most vulgar, unamused, yet unsurprised non-spoken statement that I'd ever seen.

After just a few whispers, the District Managers fell silent. They looked around the room at all of us and lined up across the wall. One after another, they looked at each other and tried to quietly decide who would be the person to deliver the news. A few moments went by before Danielle, a neighboring district manager, spoke up.

"Okay, guys..." she said, "it seems that there has been a slight change of plans."

Katty's palm splattered against her face like a paintball, but I could tell she knew she had to keep quiet about what was going on. Whatever they were about to say was going to be complete horse-shit, and I could tell by the look on her face that she knew it. What was she going to do, though? Tell her bosses that their *only job* was to forward emails and *even then* they were a few screws short of a hardware store? Yeah. It was obvious that she had to keep her trap shut. Katty's ability to remain quiet, however, didn't set any spectacular standards.

"Who forgot to check their email?" she asked.

Danielle was stopped in her tracks. After a few seconds of silence, Mitch decided to step in and help her out.

"Great call-out, Katty. It turns out that the time has been

changed from noon to one o'clock," he said. "The change was…
unforeseen, but—manageable."

Another district manager decided to continue, "We'll start
organizing and preparing in about fifteen minutes… to save
some time."

Danielle once again decided to cue in, "Efficiency is key."

Katty let out an audible groan as I started connecting the
dots. Janice originally told me that it started at one o'clock, but
just that morning she called and told me that *Mitch told her* that
it started at noon. Since all of the MAPP candidates were waiting
for nearly an hour and all of the other store managers showed up
around the right time, it started to look like the time was changed
to one o'clock after the district managers were told about it—it
became apparent that an area-wide email was sent but most of the
district managers neglected to check it.

So, when they called all of their store managers to remind
them, they gave them the wrong time.

After they concluded their little chat with us, the district
managers talked amongst themselves for a good few minutes
about whether or not MAPP was paid, and they concluded that it
was. The frightful thought of all the labor dollars they were going
to waste started to cross their minds, and they promptly turned
back toward the table in unison.

"Let's get started. Efficiency is key," they said and put that last statement on repeat, "efficiency is key."

It was only about ten minutes of printing itineraries and shuffling around paperwork before the door opened. The remaining district managers walked, in followed closely by Lindsay.

Lindsay stood powerfully in the center of all of them. She flaunted her white, teethy grin, presumably to show us that *no*, she was *not* going to eat us alive. However, the wrinkles and shadows under her eyes portrayed the exact opposite idea. We may not be eaten, but by the time we left we'd most certainly be dead.

Since Lindsay hadn't met any of us except merely in passing, she decided to make a general call to everyone in the group.

"Okay, ladies and gentlemen. Welcome to MAPP," she said. "Who all do we have here? Let's start with you, on this side of the table, and we can work our way around."

Just as the shift supervisor on the other side of the table started to talk, Lindsay interrupted her.

"Just say your first name, where you're from, and what your store has been up to," she said.

The shift supervisor waited a few moments and nervously

introduced herself, followed quickly by the person next to her, then so on and so forth. It felt like the red squadron pilot team reporting in on their way toward the Death Star. One at a time, everyone introduced themselves, all in a terrified yet frightfully optimistic tone.

"Red 5 standing by."

"Red Dawn standing by."

"Reddit.com standing by."

After a short few seconds, it got to me. I took a breath and put my best foot forward.

"I'm Tony," I said, "I work at the Deuce location, I've been a shift manager for over a year, I'm working an overnight later today, and let me tell you... being here is *absolutely swell.*"

I was never all that great at introductions.

Granted, neither were they. You know, with all that "Red" nonsense.

The questions at the table were dull and centralized on common topics. *Can anyone tell the best way to repair the relationship with an unsatisfied customer? What does B.L.A.S.T. stand for? What's the process on proofing pizzas? Let's say you're in the weeds and a customer enters the restaurant and places a*

volume order, what's the P.U.R.E. thing to do?

Other shift managers would chime in to answer but it would take them a small few seconds and when they did, they sounded worried. Lindsay *preyed* on fear. When one of my comrades answered without a misguided air of confidence, she'd interrupt them and pick out every little detail about their opportunities. When one of us would act proudly about our answer, however, she'd compliment us and ask the next question, regardless of how wrong we were. After a while, it started to look like it was a competition for who could speak up the most and answer the loudest, so when it came to corporate vomit and speaking out of turn, I became *king.*

I felt like an *asshole.* I looked at the table around me and saw the resigned look on the faces of all the other shift managers. I wished that I could stop and help them. I wished that I could pause time and tell them to speak up and apologize for being so... *obscene.* I felt especially bad for Barbara, who was promoted to shift manager around the same time as I was.

I was borrowed for their store for a week or so a few months back, so I had gotten to know the team pretty well. She was a single mom of two kids and had to live with her roommate in a two-bedroom apartment. She had no family, no friends that were willing to jump in and help, no one. She needed this promotion more than I did, there was no doubt in my mind, and I could tell that she wanted it. Every time I stopped for a moment to let her answer a question, though, she'd either wait too long and someone else would interrupt her or she'd answer nervously and Lindsay would come back so hard on her that it was borderline offensive. I... *didn't have a choice.* I had to keep pressing on. The only positive was the sheer amount of praise I was getting from Lindsay, which to be fair, wasn't even aimed at me. Every time I'd answer, she'd give me some compliment about how I was quick on my feet or a perfect example of a P.U.R.E. candidate—and then she'd turn to Mitch and compliment *him.*

"I'm so glad your district is setting everyone up for success, Mitch! You're setting a great example here!"

It wasn't long after the questions were finished being asked that it was time to go on a floor walk. Lindsay picked up the stack of papers that we were working on when we first got there and gave them to the shift manager next to her.

"Take one and pass it on," she said.

As everyone was taking and passing, she stood at the front of the table and told us what exactly we'd be doing with those sheets.

"Alright, so have any of you seen these before?" she asked.

Most of us nodded.

I looked toward her, smiled, and said, *"Of course!"*—because I'm a fucking asshat.

"Excellent," she said.

Looking down at my paper, I started to look over the sheet. Floor-walk forms are pretty simple. They have a list of areas around the store, dishwasher area, computer desk, front counter, Teamwork Tomato wall, and several others, and a rating tool next to them

"Alright, everyone!" she said, "let's follow Mitch!"

Mitch looked up and gave Lindsay a confused grin.

"Mitch, could you do me a favor and walk everyone down the street to the restaurant?" she asked.

"Definitely," he said. "Does everyone have a pen?"

Very few of us had pens. He took a moment to aimlessly search for a box. No luck. He tried searching a little harder, checking drawers and cabinets, until he realized that Lindsay was giving him an awful stare.

"No problem," he said, "they'll have some pens for us there."

Everyone stood up and formed a line like a bunch of kindergarteners. Once everyone was in place, we started to march out.

"Oh, Tony," Lindsay said.

This couldn't be good.

"Instead of going with them to the restaurant, do you think we could have a little chat first?"

Oh shit. This *wasn't* good.

"Mitch, we'll meet you guys over there," she said in a way that sounded more like a question than a statement.

Mitch nodded and walked everyone out until it was just me. Alone. With Lindsay. I felt like the kids in that kitchen scene of Jurassic Park. For a second, all I could do was stare at her. I felt my heart throbbing, trying its best to jump out of my chest so that maybe I wouldn't have to be alive when she picked the meat from my bones.

What could she possibly want with me? Was I being too loud during the group interview? Oh shit, I *was* being too loud. Or maybe she wanted to talk about last Tuesday? Whatever it was, I was sure it wasn't good.

"Don't worry. It will only take a few minutes," she said, and indicated with her hand that she wanted me to follow her.

Leaving the conference room, we headed down the corridor and past a group of offices. Most of the doors were shut, presumably because the district managers were out walking with the shift managers. As we walked, I tried to read the name plates on each one to see if I could find Mitch's office, but I couldn't see it.

Eventually we made it to Lindsay's office. She opened the door for me and I walked inside. The office was huge. The walls were filled with bookshelves and motivational posters, the desk stretched out seemingly infinitely across the room, and behind her chair was a large window featuring the parking lot below.

"Thank you for coming all this way out here, Tony," she said. "I know it's a long way from the Deuce location."

"Oh," I said, trying not to sound anxious, "it was no problem at all. I'm happy to be here."

"Well, Tony, one day, I'm hoping that this drive won't be too out of the ordinary," she said.

Huh?

We both sat down.

"I see a lot of potential in you, Tony," Lindsay said. "As you know, whenever we conduct a MAPP session, I make sure to look through the records of all of the talent before they arrive."

I nodded.

"Last Tuesday, you received a few complaints. One of them called Mitch directly. Do you remember Blake? He had a volume order that he placed within the store. He informed Mitch that the order was completed nearly an hour after he ordered it, so I took the liberty of pulling the order up and calling him back myself."

Volume order?—Oh, wait. That *twenty-seven pizza* guy. God. *Dammit.*

"Now, before you say anything, he was perfectly understanding on the phone. He told us that he just wanted to inform us that you may need just a little more training," she said.

"I did give him a credit for the full amount of his purchase, which I'm sure you offered him as well, but in the end, he was completely satisfied."

I found everything that she was saying *impossible* to believe and I didn't know what to say.

"Well," I started and had no clue how to finish, "I'm glad he left happy. That was my goal."

"I can tell," she said. "I looked at your schedule for that day and gathered that you were pretty understaffed. I just wanted to pull you in and talk to you about that, just to let you know that he ended up leaving happy. I also just wanted to give you some feedback and let you know that you should never give the customer any reason to believe that you're short-handed. If you plan on staying with Pizza Corp and moving up the corporate ladder, which I'm sure you do, I think our highest priority needs to be your customer focus. There are training courses on this topic when you go to assistant manager training, and trust me, you won't believe how much you'll learn when you get there."

I nodded again, feeling the gravity press me further into the chair and trying my damnedest to keep proper posture.

"That's all I wanted to talk to you about for now," she said. "So how are things going on the frontlines? How is Janice adjusting to her role?"

This went on for a little while. We wrapped up with a thirty-minute discussion solely in corporate jargon. The conversation went as follows, courteously translated into proper English:

"How's the store?" she asked.

"It sucks, but we're trying to make it less shitty," I said.

"Great!" she said. "You'll do it eventually."

"[Insert explanation of "P.U.R.E." and exclamation of how impressive Pizza Corp culture is here.] Pizza Corp is quite the company!" I said.

Eventually, it was all over. We walked back to the conference room and greeted everyone else. I asked Lindsay if I should go for a store-walk by myself, but she smiled and told me that everything was already handled, whatever that meant. The shift managers formed a line and shook hands with the district managers, and then we all walked out of the office and went home. In a way, it was less painful than I imagined.

I was done.

Holy hell, I was *done.* I didn't have to worry about that shit anymore. I mean sure, it wasn't really done. Trinity still had cancer, we were still behind on bills, and I still had to be incident free until my score from MAPP was decided. But, I mean, still. That was a huge weight lifted from my shoulders. Even though I knew that my MAPP scores, whatever they were, weren't going to attribute to my main problems, I found it in myself to be happy about the fact that I didn't have to worry about them anymore.

When I got back to the house, I turned on my computer and Trinity and I played some video games. I didn't have that many, nothing new anyway, but we took turns playing BioShock until she fell asleep next to me. After a while, I turned the game off and just looked at her, brushing her hair with my fingers. It was nice seeing her finally look rested again, even if it was only when she was sleeping. I placed my lips on the shadows under her eyes and pretended that I could just kiss the pain away. At around eleven-thirty, I carefully got up, gently put her head on the pillow, and draped the blanket over her.

That was all I got. That was all I *ever* got. A few quick moments here and there. That small glass of water was all I had to fill the whole ocean, and no matter how hard I tried, it could only be half-full. Standing up, looking at her untroubled, tranquil face, I convinced myself that after everything worked out... *however it worked out...* I'd get to spend more time with her. I told myself that when we grew up together, when our children had children, when all we had to worry about was what we needed to get from the grocery store, we'd look back and forget all this. One day, this would all be over.

But that day was not today.

I separated myself from my longing, wishful thoughts. I got my clothes back on, turned the lights off, and headed back out to Pizza Corp.

I pulled up into the parking lot and let the car coast into the parking space. Taking a long, deep, relaxed breath, I prepared myself for the trip inside. I knew there wasn't going to be anyone there, except maybe Janice if she was still there after having opened that morning. That's right, Janice opened *and* closed. She was bound to ask how MAPP went. I didn't feel like it went poorly but I just didn't have the energy to walk her through my day. What was I going to tell her?

I lifted my head back up and looked toward Pizza Corp.

The lights were off. No one was there. Good.

I let out a small sigh. I didn't have to talk to anyone. It was just me and Max. Tonight was going to be easy. I was sure that Janice was going to leave me a note telling me to deep clean something to make myself useful while the crew was cleaning the oven, but at least the work wouldn't be tedious. I could just start on it, work on it, and then go home. All I had to do was wait for Max.

Making another sigh, I looked at my phone. Midnight on

the dot. Where was she? I poked my head around and looked through the back windows and immediately felt like a jerk. There she was, sitting on the curb by the back door, throwing rocks into Sonic's parking lot. How long had she been waiting there?

I gathered my energy and pulled myself out of the car.

"Hey," I said, walking up to her.

I took a seat on the cement next to her. She looked toward me, forced a smile, and looked back toward the night sky. She put the cigarette up to her lips and inhaled like an industrial vacuum cleaner.

"You okay?" I asked.

She sighed.

"Yeah," she said, "just a little stressed."

"What's up?" I asked her.

She threw another rock and put out what little of the cigarette was left. She took a breath and started to say something but retracted it.

"It's just…" she said, "I don't know. My account is sitting at negative ninety-seven bucks and I promised day care that I'd pay them tomorrow and my car payment for a car that I don't even have is a month behind. I don't even drive that car. That car and I aren't even in the same state. For the last few days when I woke up, I looked at my phone and read an alert that said my bank charged me another thirty dollars in overdrafts. It started off at six dollars in the red. Six. And now I'm at negative ninety-seven. I thought I was finally caught up… but I'm not."

She sighed.

"It's just a lot, you know?" she said.

I wanted to tell her that *yeah, I knew,* but the truth of the matter was that I didn't know. I had my own struggles, sure, but our two situations were so immensely different. Not only that, but the way we processed them was different. I tried to ignore my problems and pretend that they didn't exist… while Max actively tried to overcome them. She tried, holding nothing back, to figure out every last detail. I admired that about her. She was always thinking. Her mind was always sprinting, trying desperately to figure out a solution to every problem… even if she was fully aware that there wasn't one.

"You ready?" I asked.

She nodded.

I stood up, reached out my hand toward her, and pulled her up.

I pushed the door open slowly. It was pitch black. Walking in, my foot banged against the case holding the pizza boxes. I figured Janice would at least leave the light on for us.

We turned the lights on and started to get settled. Max plugged her adapter into the console and sat down at table one. The building was dead quiet. It was nerve-wrenching and awkward. Typically, even though we turn the oven off when we leave the store every night after close, it's still in its cooling process by the time we walk out the door. That thing was always making noise. Same with the fryer and all of our other equipment. There are so many buzzing noises, beeps, creaks and clicks that you start not to notice any of them anymore. But during an overnight shift, everything is off. You can hear the cockroaches crawl across the floor. It's borderline terrifying.

After about fifteen minutes, I went to the back of the store—you know, to check store email, make sure all of the invoices were put in correctly, the works—and after few moments of silence, my phone vibrated. A text from Trinity.

"Can you steal me another delivery bag?" her message said, "I'm baking my mom some lasagna for her work meeting tomorrow."

Okay, yes, I know. Stealing is a bad, bad thing.

"We have like ten of them already. Why don't you use those?" I typed.

"They're all in your car," she responded.

"I put one in yours," I typed. "You know. Just in case. :)"

The message showed that it was read for a few minutes... and then she responded again.

"This is why I married you," the message said.

"I love you too," I told her.

I went back up to the front of the store and sat down with Max. The oven-cleaning crew usually showed up a few hours late. I guess I couldn't blame them. They had all night and it was not like we weren't going to be there to let them in.

At first, Max and I didn't say much. She didn't even have her music playing yet. The silence was nice in a weird sort of way. After the week that we'd had, with all of the loud customers, the noisy machinery, and everything else... having nothing to listen or pay attention to was great.

Just sitting there, looking at the table, Max held her own hands.

"I think that I... I have to schedule his surgery. Don't I?" she asked. "Soon?"

It took me a few more seconds.

"I thought you said that you already scheduled it," I said.

She took another breath and held it long enough to stop her heart from breaking from her chest.

"I... I brought cards," she said.

She turned around and started digging into her backpack. Pulling the cards out, she removed them from the box and gently sat them on the table. Holding all four sides with her fingers trying to keep them steady so they didn't move a single bit, her fingers shook ever so slightly and knocked some to the side.

"Max," I said.

"Did you know that every time you shuffle a deck of cards, it's pretty likely that it shuffles in an order that the universe has never seen?" she said.

"How do you mean?" I asked.

"Well," she said, "there are only fifty-two cards, but statistically it's enough to be almost truly random. I read somewhere that no two decks are shuffled the same. From the eighteen hundreds all the way until now. Each shuffle is different."

"That's interesting," I said, "But... Max—"

"—Have you ever wondered what it would've been like if our decks were shuffled differently?" she said and drew a card from the top.

I took one as well. I didn't know why.

"What's yours?" she asked.

I placed it on the table. King of Hearts.

Ever since I was a kid," she said, "when it was time to put the cards up I always put the Queen of Spades next to the King of Hearts and put them on top. I don't know why. I just remember a teacher telling me in, like, second grade, that each time a deck is shuffled it's different and it'll never be the same again."

"So, you've got the Queen of Spades?" I asked. "Why those two? Why not the clubs or diamonds?"

"I don't know," she said. "I guess I just always thought that even though the rest of the deck is different, these two will be the same. And, maybe... I don't know."

"Yeah you do," I said. "Maybe...?"

"Maybe..." she said, "maybe those two, in some way, would set a good example somehow. I don't know. I was a kid."

She sighed.

"I'm sorry," she said. "I—I'm just going to shut up. I'm exhausted and I'm blabbering out jibberish."

She started to put the cards back in the box, but I put my hand out to stop her.

"No," I said. "Hold on."

It started to occur to me that maybe she didn't have anyone to talk to either. Maybe that was why she was always nervous and jittery. She held everything in. She was doing everything herself. Even though she saw people, maybe she never opened up to them. Maybe the only reason she talked to me about anything was because she needed to. I guess it didn't matter. I enjoyed listening, no matter where any of this went.

"So..." I said, "maybe the rest of them would, no pun intended, follow suit?"

"I guess so," she said, "yeah."

I stayed silent and just looked into her blue eyes, both of which were looking far away from mine. I just wanted her to keep going. All I had was bits and pieces of her story. I wanted not only the full painting, but the whole gallery. I knew, though, that at best I had to settle for a brush-stroke.

"What if..." she said, "what if this life is just one of many? What if we have an infinite number of lives? What if we're twos and threes now and, maybe in the next life, we'll be kings and queens?"

"You're talking about reincarnation?" I asked.

"Kind of," she said. "I don't know, don't listen to me. I'm tired."

"No, no." I said, urgently, "go on. Please."

"Well," she said, "what if life is really what we make it? What if, every time you're passionate about an idea, it comes true in another universe? What if, maybe, in that universe, you can shuffle the deck however you want it?"

She shrugged.

"Maybe... one day, we'll wake up and all of our problems will just be gone. What if we can go to college, our families can be healthy, and we can *just... live our lives.* What if... what if there are infinite possibilities, infinite shuffles, and we're just cards in the deck?"

Her oceanic eyes hit mine and lit up my heart like a bottle rocket in a smoke-filled night sky.

"Do you believe in alternate worlds, Tony?" she asked.

It took me a moment to figure out how to respond. I didn't

want to say no, but how could I say yes? Here was something that she had been thinking about since she was a kid and at first glance I was supposed to just be completely on board? I guess she didn't actually expect me to think that way. I just didn't know what she thought or what she wanted... Maybe she didn't know either. Neither of us got any sleep. We couldn't think clearly. These were dream-thoughts that no one was meant to understand. This was pure emotion in the form of a conversation.

Slowly, calmly, I put the King of Hearts into the center of the deck and shuffled it in just the way that it would end up near the top. Placing the deck back on the table, I started to flip the cards one at a time.

"I believe..." I said, flipping the Two of Clubs, Six of Diamonds, then Four of Spades, "I guess I believe in the world I was dealt to, Max."

King of Hearts.

"We just haven't hit the top yet," I told her.

She let out a long sigh and started putting the cards back in the box, making sure to put the King of Hearts and Queen of Spades on top.

"I mean," I said, "you don't think that the guy at 365 Emerald Circle is the freaking King of Hearts, do you?"

She shrugged and shuffled through her backpack again.

"I mean," she said, "maybe not. But he's sure doing better

than us."

"For now," I said and made a sarcastic grin. "But you know, Max, with a little bit of teamwork, delegation and efficiency—"

"*Oh my god,*" she laughed, "I don't want to hear it."

I chuckled.

A few moments later, we fell silent again. She put her hands up to her face, wiped some of her dripping makeup from her eyes, and looked at it on her hands.

"I must look pathetic," she said.

"Why do you say that?" I asked.

She shuffled a bit, trying to stop herself from having another attack. "You said something in corporate lingo to cheer me up. I know you're full of that shit, but I've never seen you let any of it leak out."

"Hey now. Corporate lingo isn't *that* bad," I lied.

"Oh, whatever," she said. "You know better than I do that it's just a bunch of powerful sounding words thrown together in order to sound smart and say nothing."

I nodded, trying my best to keep my grin.

"Oh, you're not wrong," I said.

"So, I'm right," she said.

"Well… no," I said. "Not really."

She gave me a look that she only gives faulty kitchen timers and people who order vegetarian pizzas but add pepperoni.

"Go on," she said, squinting her eyes and leaning forward.

"Corporate-speak doesn't have to be just powerful sounding words strung together with no meaning. If it's used properly, it can be poetic. Think Star Trek," I said. "Without all that corporate labor-saving junk, teamwork and synergy actually have meaning. The reason I hate it so much is how often they use it improperly."

"Oh, please," she said. "Tell me one thing in corporate-speak that sounds *beautiful.*"

I sifted my fingers through my hair and closed my eyes, pulling back the memories of something from long ago.

Feeling her hand gently caress my arm, my eyes jolted open. Max, still sitting across from me, leaned her body over the table in the most provocative position possible, licked her lips and pushed her shoulders inward letting her breasts shine through the top of her blouse.

Was she flirting with me? Or was she just comfortable enough with her body that she felt like she could do this as a joke?

"Talk corporate to me, Tony," she said with a chuckle.

It *was* a joke. Maintaining that shit-eating grin, her icy eyes gleamed toward my flabbergasted face.

"So?" she said.

I bit my lip and thought about how to start.

She lifted her eyebrow.

I sighed.

"Tell us about our opportunities," I quoted a dream-thought that I'd written down a long, long time ago. "But not how to *fix* them, how to *achieve* them. We want more than to *advance our career* here. We want to *retire* from here."

She stared.

I stared back, embarrassed.

"Go on," she said.

"Let's achieve our life's best work. Here. Now," I recited. "Become the person we never thought we could be, and then improve some more. Together, we'll make achieving our dreams a dull event from a distant past. Then we'll clock in and go even further."

Her head rested on the palms of her hands as she stared into my words.

"And then," I said, "after everything, we'll achieve *even more* for *someone else.*"

She gave me a smile.

"What's that from?" she asked.

I turned away, embarrassed. I wasn't sure if I could tell her. But there we were. I'd shared it with her already. She'd heard it. I had no choice but to open myself up.

"Before I came back to Pizza Corp, I worked at a small accounting firm," I said. "The CPA asked me to make a mission statement."

"Did they use it?" she asked.

I shook my head.

"No," I said. "They went with something about client profits and valuing their bottom line."

She sighed.

"Well..." she said, "I know I'd do *anything* for *that* kind of company."

"Assuming it exists," I said.

She nodded.

"It does," she said.

I sighed and looked deep into her eyes.

"Who knows?" I said. "Maybe after a few more shuffles, we'll get to see it firsthand."

Without warning, I heard music blast from the kitchen. I jumped, shocked, until I realized that it was just Max streaming it from her phone. Turning back toward her, I felt the table wobble as she climbed up on top of it and reached her hand out to me.

"Want to dance?" she asked.

I took her hand.

We danced.

Act 3

CHAPTER 7

This is what a gummy worm looks like:

You know, just in case you forgot. It's been a while. Actually, a few months have passed... a lot's happened since then. Sure, not enough to have documented every last detail with my trademark sarcastic yet charming verbosity, but surely enough for you to wish that I had. For starters, the ball started rolling on the corporate side of our "Pizza Corp Journey." It turns out that nobody is allowed to know our MAPP results except for the people a step above us. Janice ended up telling me Max's score, so of course, like the gentleman I am, I told Max. After that, somehow George found out, and even though he no longer worked for Pizza Corp, he made sure that everyone else knew. After a while, Janice decided that since everyone was going to find out one way or another, she'd tell me what mine was as well. We both got a two. We're badass.

Max's process went relatively quickly. Mitch voiced his hesitation to Lindsay, but the conversation went quickly and decisively in Max's favor.

Here's the play-by-play:
1. Lindsay told Mitch that she loved Max's interview.
2. Mitch was concerned with his district-wide D.R.I.V.E. scores.
3. Lindsay told Mitch to promote her anyway.
4. Mitch refused.

5. Lindsay called Mitch into her office.

6. (This one's the game-changer) When Mitch sat down, Lindsay printed a stack of emails from Mitch to HR to assist in the recruiting process of shift managers. She then printed a list of employee survey results lasting Mitch's entire employment with Pizza Corp, all stating that the biggest disappointment was promotional opportunities. She stapled all of this to Mitch's yearly self-review and locked the door to her office.

7. Hilarity ensued.

According to Katty, it was only a few hours later that Mitch called Max and offered her the position. Now this is all hearsay, rumors from Katty down to us, but I'm choosing to believe it. It's nice to see the system work in a meaningful way for once. I say meaningful; more like begrudgingly conclusive. Still, it's nice to see some sort of decisive corporate action happening.

At the time, it was great. We didn't know where she would end up, just about every store needed a shift manager, but we didn't care. We were all happy for her.

And then, just a few days later, Max went to training. She never came back to our store.

As much as I'd like to deny it, at first I didn't notice. It was just another day. Nothing changed. Business as usual. It was just work, you know? I went in, worked a shift, and left. Max just didn't work that day. After a while, it just slipped out of thought. It just wasn't something that we thought about.

Like I once said, that's the thing with the service industry. People leave. No one gives it a second thought. There's no goodbye, there's never a hug or any final words. Nothing. It's just another day at work. Even with the people you care about, after they clock out for the last time, they're gone. However, once in a blue moon, there's someone who seems to take a piece of you with them.

No one notices that anything's changed until there's a small reminder: a specific order, a left-behind name-badge, a broken picture frame... that stupid "Ring for Service" bell.

Right at open, I sat with my stack of resumes getting ready to conduct some interviews, and someone started chiming that fucking bell. Memories hit me like a train. Max's backpack, her music, the awkward twitch of her hands when she got nervous, Dominic playing with the damn bell... and without hesitation I shot my eyes up to take a look at the counter to see if just maybe she was standing there...

... It wasn't Max. Just some asshole customer.

Of course it was. She'd moved on. She had finished training by then I was sure, but wherever she ended up, she was definitely happier than she had been here... and as much as I'd have loved to see her, I was glad that *she wasn't here.* And I was glad I'd had some hand in helping her get wherever her life took her.

Anyway, for the moment, life had taken *me* to this table, where I was sorting papers.

This is what a paperclip looks like:

Paperclips are small, metallic objects that are used with a stack of papers to, you know, *keep them in a stack.* They're useful when keeping track of documents, packets, or—

—*Yeah... you know what a paperclip is.*

sigh

I was out of paperclips and had too many papers, so I ended up stacking them and folding the top-right corners as a kind of bookmark. Most of the applications and interview sheets were already filled out, so that made it easier. There was one stack that was completely blank, though. It didn't even have a name.

Janice was about to leave for a week. She was being borrowed by another store a few cities away, meaning that until she got back, I was in charge of the hiring. Most of it was done for me. She had already scheduled all of the interviews and put them into the system. All I had to do was interview and click "hire." Should be easy, right?

Nope. These interviews looked like they were scheduled at the last minute. Like I said before, one of them didn't even have a name attached to it. What was she thinking, that I'd just magically know who it was that I was interviewing?—I guessed it'd be obvious. If a person was here seeking an interview and he or she wasn't already listed on the other papers, it would have to be the no-name person, right?

My mind started to drift. It was easy to get distracted. After a bit, I started thinking about life on the home front. Although I had scored a two, no offers for assistant manager came my way. It figures, I guess. Pizza Corp always needs more shift managers and HR always has external applications flooding out their nose. At first, the spot at my store was filled by an external hire named Roderick, who was hired for $31,000 a year and never came to training. Following that, they hired Michael. He was given $35,000 a year. He went through the four weeks of training and worked at the store for three weeks before he quit. During this whole process, I emailed Mitch, resubmitted my resume, found a way to get recommendations from Janice, Katty, and Max. No response from Mitch until one day, during a conference call, he told me that he dissolved the position.

... And then, two weeks later, Crabby accepted *her* offer.

It was official—without a single interview, Crabby was the new assistant manager. I guess I wasn't surprised. After Mitch dissolved the position, there was an uproar among the store managers in our district. Everyone was worried that if *they* had a vacant position, *it might dissolve as well.* Mitch, stuck between a rock and a throw-pillow, *eventually chose the rock* and gave it to someone he'd seen manage the store before—then promptly dissolved Crabby's old position. So, in all reality, nothing really had changed.

A month or so had passed since then before Mitch, apparently under a lot of pressure to meet sales and labor goals for his district, filed his two-weeks notice. It didn't take Lindsay long to replace him. From the sound of it, it was a long time coming. After five or so weeks of training, we got to meet our shiny new district manager.

Kyle.

I'd go into describing his physical attributes and personality, but really, as far as district managers go, you get the idea. It's all the same.

Regardless, this was exactly what I wanted. I was off to a fresh start. The only thing this guy knew about me was that I had three recommendations from highly recognized employees and I had scored a two at MAPP. It was fantastic. In fact, during his first week on the job, he came by to give our store a walk. I was actually on the clock that day, which I'm sure was no mistake by Janice. When he came by, he dedicated thirty minutes out of his day to talk to me, which was a pleasant surprise.

The conversation went like this:

Kyle: Hello! I'm Kyle! I'm a corporate tool. I'd like to be your friend!

Me: Nice to meet you, Kyle! I'm Tony! I really need a promotion. Has anyone ever told you that your asshole smells fantastic?

Kyle: Thanks for that feedback, Tony! I've been really trying to hammer out that area. I was thinking about spraying a thick coat of strawberry-vanilla up there. What's your input on that?

Me: Whatever you have going on right now works great, however I do think a light coat of strawberry-vanilla might just do the trick. It's a bit feng shui though, you don't want your asshole to blend in. Start off strong and let us ease into it.

Kyle: Those are some excellent points, Tony. I'll be sure to add this conversation into your Personal Development Plan!

A few days later I was able to pull up my PDP; sure enough, in the management comments section, after all of my reviews and recommendations was a comment from Kyle.

That comment went like this:

Kyle: Tony pointed out that my asshole smells fantastic! He recommended that I ease into a strawberry-vanilla scent. That's some keen knowledge that could only come from the most experienced talent. We have some positions opening up, so I'm taking some time aside to schedule another MAPP session for him. Great job, Tony!

I was pretty optimistic.

Organizing the blank papers, I tried to make sense of the whole thing. Wait. It had a *time.* Ten o'clock. The fuck? Whoever this interview was with, it was scheduled first thing in the morning—right... *now?*

I pulled out my phone to check the time.

Five minutes ago, actually.

Outstanding. We were off to a great start.

I felt a tap on the right shoulder and turned to greet whoever it was. There was no one there. Oh, this guy thinks he's so clever. I turned around and looked to my left but before I could fully turn my head, I saw George in the corner of my eye sitting down across from me.

"How's it going, BossMan?" he said.

I shrugged.

"Hey man. Janice isn't here right now. She's at another store," I told him as I looked back to the papers. "I'm actually doing an early interview right now. If you give me a minute to verify that this person is not showing up, I'll be right with you."

George dropped something onto the table. With my attention focused on the sheets in front of me, I couldn't see what it was. That is, until he slid it over to me and flicked it down on top of the interview papers.

"Sorry BossMan," he said. "That guy's here right now."

I held out my hand and he gave me the plastic card. It was his work visa.

Hey, alright!

Up until that point, I'd never actually seen a work visa before. It's about what you'd expect it to look like. Government issued, sloppily laminated, terrible formatting, and a picture of George just at the moment when he was least ready for the camera. To the camera's credit, George never looked ready for any camera. His eyes sunk so far into his head and his ears were so gigantic that every portrait of his face made him look like Andross from the Star Fox games.

"I was actually here on time but I didn't want to ring the stupid bell like that asshole did," he said and pointed to the customer at the counter. I watched for a few moments to make sure he was being helped. Reece eventually made his way up to greet him.

Fair enough, I thought.

"So, you're here for an interview," I said. "Next time, apply online. It's more accurate that way. We're not hiring right now."

He scoffed at me.

"Whatever, BossMan," he said. "Janice couldn't get the people that said they were processing my stuff to actually process my stuff. So she told me that she was going to hire me as a re-hire, so they had to process my stuff. Apparently they will process applicants faster than everyone else. Go figure. She called me yesterday and let me know so I could come in for my interview."

Huh. So that was why none of this was filled out. I guessed that Janice was covering her ass in case there was a surprise visit.

"So... you've already gotten the job, huh?" I asked.

"Apparently," he said.

While I read through his work visa, George plopped something else down on the table in front of me.

"Also," he said, "this is for you, BossMan."

I reached over and picked it up. It was a Teamwork Tomato.

This is what it looked like:

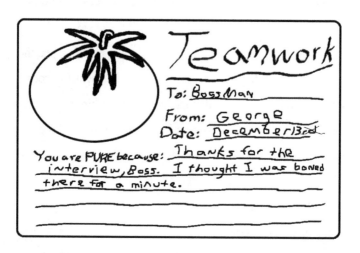

"How did you have this filled out already?" I asked. "Did you sneak behind the counter before you talked to me?"

George shook his head.

"No, BossMan," he said, "I stole one of those giant packs of them when you guys fired me. I've been giving them out to everyone."

I smiled, rolled my eyes, and imagined George giving one to his aunt for going out of her way to attend a family holiday party.

I looked at my notes for this interview. Managers have three packets of interview questions for new hires. One's for first-time employees, that's the easiest one. One's for employees with experience, which is a little harder—and then we have an older, generic list of questions, which is the hardest. Some of the questions on that one are just mean. By default, I usually grab the easy one because, what the hell, interviews rarely tell us what we need to know. I just look for how much effort they're putting into answering the questions. This time, though, I figured I'd have a little fun.

"I'll be right back," I said, "I need to print out the interview sheet."

"But you already—" he said and immediately caught on. "Hold on! Let's wait a minute!"

With a conceited grin on my face, I sat back down across the table from him. He grimaced at me the same way that a cat would toward the human that took his freshly-caught bird.

"Alright, so this is going to be a quick and easy process," I said, giving him my usual rigmarole. "I'm going to start by asking a few standard questions. All of them are predetermined, so they may seem a little strange, but just roll with it and don't worry."

"Yeah, thanks BossMan," he said.

I had given him his first interview. He knew how this went. It was just fun putting him through the shit again.

"Do you have any questions so far?" I asked.

He thought about it for a second.

"Yeah, so a few weeks ago I was chilling in the lobby waiting for Janice and a guy came in. He ordered a pizza with buffalo sauce on it. And Reece was all like, 'Yeah sure, we can do that!' But what the hell, we can't do that! Can we?" he said.

"Actually," I started, "there's a new special that—"

"And who puts buffalo sauce on a pizza?!" he said. "That doesn't make any sense. Next we'll be putting Garlic Parmesan on salads and ranch on pasta... and marinara on chicken wings or something."

"Okay, so first question," I told him after a good ten minutes of listening to him blabber about buffalo sauce, "can you name a time that you admitted a mistake or failure?"

This was my favorite interview question of all time. Occasionally I would choose the hard set of interview questions just so I could ask it.

He thwacked the table with conviction.

"Remember that time," he started.

Okay, let's stop for a moment. When asked to name a time that you've admitted a mistake or failure, it's never... *never* a good idea to start the answer with, "*remember that time.*"

Alright, let's continue.

"Remember that time when that customer called and complained that their pizza was cold and you were like, 'Oh man, I'm sorry sir' and made me send them another pizza? And then when they got that second pizza, they called again and said it was cold, so you made me send them *another* pizza?" he asked.

"*Yes. . .*"I said.

"And then remember how I was all like, 'Yeah Tony, I'm making sure this pizza is cold this time because this guy is an asshole for complaining so many times?' So then I opened up the box in the car and pointed the air conditioner at it so that it'd be freezing?" he asked.

"*Yes. . .*"I said again.

"Yeah, well, it was probably cold that first time. That delivery was already a miss and I stopped by that snow cone place and got myself something on the way," he said.

"George," I said, "what the hell. I told you to name a time when you admitted a mistake or a failure. You never told me this!"

"Well I just did!" he said. "Now's a time that I'm admitting a mistake or a failure. Seriously, Tony. You asked for a story of a time that I did something and I'm giving you the most relevant example."

I immediately got up, saying nothing, went to the back of house computer, and printed the easy interview sheets.

... And I *still* had to fudge most of his answers.

A few hours later, the rush was in full momentum. Customers who had previously been helped were waiting for their food, none of them looked patient. In the front of the line was a man wearing freshly gelled hair, brand-name sunglasses, a perfectly ironed polo with tightly pressed khaki pants and spit-shined shoes. I greeted him and he returned my greeting with a shit-eating grin that you'd expect from a sketchy used car salesman. *Businessman.*

"So here's the deal," he said.

Oh, this should be good.

"My company orders pizza for this event once a month, every month. We always order the same thing. Ten pepperoni, ten sausage, ten cheese, ten vegetarian, and twelve two-liters of soda. We always have it delivered to the same place at the same time," he said, flailing his arms and pointing at me with the top of his name-brand cell-phone. "Last time, *you* were fifteen minutes late, which meant that *our clients* were present during the display setup. Now, you're a fellow businessman, you know how important appearance is. I spent hours on the phone with you guys—*hours*—and I finally spoke with someone who's name was..."

He flipped through his email on his continuously ringing phone.

"... Mitch. And he gave us a credit for the full amount. Now, our catering department neglected to order this in advance, so here I am. I've got my Camaro ready. I've got..."

He checked his smart-watch.

"... an hour and twelve minutes before the presentation starts," he said. "My trunk's open. Let's get one of your guys to help me load up the pizzas."

Huh.

A few things about that.

Firstly... y*eah, that's not going to happen.*

Secondly, I don't care how many rounds of Tetris you've played on that fancy smart-watch, forty pizzas and twelve bottles of soda aren't going to fit into a two-seater. I mean, seriously man. It's one thing to completely misjudge how our problems work since it's clear you've never worked in the food industry, but miscalculating the space you'd need for forty pizzas? C'mon. You've seen food before.

Thirdly, we prepped thirty-five hand-tossed pizzas for the Sunday morning rush. I'll be the first to admit that Pizza Corp

245

food is *shit* but that doesn't mean we literally squeeze it out of our ass. It has to be drenched in vegetable oil first and we have to thaw out the tomato-flavored paste. Shit takes time.

I could go all day, but let's move on.

"What do you mean you can't do it?!" he asked. "Look. I know it's usually required to place large orders at least thirty minutes out, but can you make an exception? I've got a full plate and these presentations are stressful. It's on a Sunday. Once a *month*. *On a weekend!* Can you imagine having to work a weekend every single month?!"

This guy.

I continued to tell him once more that we couldn't do what he was asking. Even if we had the prep we'd still have to, you know, *make the pizzas.* After I explained everything to him, he proceeded to get businessy.

"So, what you're saying is, I'm making an offer and you can't do the job," he said.

"I'm sorry sir," I told him, "we could potentially have that order later in the day, but in the time frame you requested, we just wouldn't have enough—"

"Well you just lost yourself a customer," he said, hoping that I'd jump to defend that *customer relationship,* "It looks like I'm going to have to take my business to another company."

Yeah, zero shits. Pizza Corp as a company will not see the

difference in that one order per month, and I certainly don't care. The less I see of this asshole, the better.

"Alright, sir," I said, "let me know if there's anything else I can do for you! In the meantime, feel free to take one of our catering menus. It'll explain everything you need to make a large catering order."

Yeah, I felt like being an asshole. In my defense, that was a word-for-word recited script from the "Repairing the Relationship" packet. I thought about adding a "Did you know about our ten dollar pizza deal?!" but I didn't feel like it. I wasn't in the mood.

I couldn't stop thinking about Trinity and all of the events that were about to happen in a few days. Long story short, Trinity's due date had already passed. A few weeks ago, I put in a request for unpaid time off which was supposed to start already and *it was approved,* but due to Janice being temporarily moved to another store, it was *revoked.* Yeah, go figure.

We eventually came up with a plan. Trinity was going to be induced on Tuesday and I had managed to convince Kyle to allow me to borrow another manager to take my shift from that day onward, so I could actually start my leave. Here was the thing, though. On Monday—*tomorrow*—Kyle was going to meet me at the store to conduct a... uh, *something* with me. He wouldn't say what it was. He seemed excited, though. *Great, right?* Well, not exactly. I had pretty mixed feelings. If it was a *final interview or something*, and all went well I'd start ASM training in less than a week. That's fifty-five required hours per week at a training store two hours away.

Yeah, I know. It was what I *wanted.* Call me needy, I was just looking forward to spending a little time with my newborn and wife. You know what—*you're right*, I need to stop complaining. I'll have a job that will support my family. My wife will only have to work part-time for us to stay afloat and we'll actually be able to function independently as adults. Years from now, this will all be worth it...

Right?

Besides, as the *acting store manager*, I had the privilege of working a morning shift! That night, we were going to Juan's church for a special holiday service. Normally I don't care about church too much. Juan was preaching, though. I'd be there to support him. Trinity was going as well, so it would be nice to spend some time with her.

"How many slices are on a medium pizza?" asked the next customer in line.

"Eight," I said.

"Oh. How many slices on a large?" she said.

"Eight," I said.

"Then what's the difference?!" she said.

Until then, I was here. Doing *this*.

After the rush was over, I got a bit of a break. I picked up my clipboard, started on all of the checklists and proceeded to pencil-whip most of them. After checking all of the temps and making sure that all of the food safety shit was out of the way, I made my way toward the back of the kitchen and checked on the prep and dishes—sure enough, none of that was done. I marked that bit as duties for the next shift *because let's face it, Crabby would've done the same thing to me*, and sat down at the computer.

I clicked on the link to the hiring website and quickly realized that George's information had already been put in. All I had to do was send it off… so I did, and with a click of a button, Luca Martinez was re-hired.

Oops—wait.

It came back with a bunch of red exclamation points and for a second a small part of me wanted to panic, but I soon realized the problem. One of the fields was empty.

Ooh, the start-date. This was interesting.

It could be anything. I could put whatever day I wanted. Ironically, there wasn't a background check, so I could literally

schedule him to start—

. . .

—Tomorrow.

I submitted it and it went through. *Awesome.* I closed out the system and powered the thing off.

Getting up, I noticed something from the corner of my eye that I hadn't seen in a long, long time. On the far corner of the desk, where the *"District Customer Experience Winner, 2001"* trophy once stood, dust was cleared off and the Batman action figure sat in its place—his arms rested on his hips, and his face stared boldly at the ceiling above—with a Teamwork Tomato resting firmly in his lap with a quote written in marker on its blank side that read, *"Or you live..."*

Yep. George was officially back.

Long story short, as far as the rest of the day went, I sat at the desk for a two-hour conference call that could've easily been an email and handed my shift off to Crabby. With a groan and a few grunts, she took the clipboard from me and I was out.

The sun hit my face as I walked out into the parking lot, which was a refreshing change. It always felt strange leaving during the day—and having what seemed like a full day ahead of me after work. *I could get used to this.*

I was excited for the night ahead of me. I was off to get Trinity, then together we were going to head to Juan's church—and hey, maybe we would have time to grab something to eat along the way. We didn't have the money for it, that was for sure, but maybe I could get away with spending ten dollars or so on some nachos...

On the way to get Trinity, my phone vibrated almost constantly. It'd been doing that for a few weeks around this time every day. *Collection agencies.* I tried answering one of the calls once and the vicious monster on the other end threatened to sue me if I didn't pay him three hundred bucks. I never answered another one, but they kept calling... every single day, never leaving a voicemail. Throughout the entire drive home, I thought of nothing but what Kyle wanted the next day. If it was another interview... would it be possible that by the end of my leave I'd finally be considered for the promotion? I guessed I'd find out eventually... Regardless, there was only one more day left—and then I wouldn't have to care anymore.

CHAPTER 8

That evening out together was fantastic. Trinity and I made it to the service just on time—we stopped by the movies first, paid for a ticket, (yes, yes, congrats again *Star Wars*) got some popcorn and nachos, then listened to NPR in the car and just ate and talked... talked about the baby, old friends, old stories, everything. For a moment, I debated just not going to church so I could spend a few more hours with her. I forgot how *fascinating* she was. She really wasn't supposed to be on her feet anyway, but to her point, she hadn't left the house in several days.

We made it to church and conducted the million obligatory handshakes—you know, church stuff—and sat down.

The first hour or so was filled with music—which wasn't as bad as I expected. Then again, I didn't know what to expect.

Once the worship music finished, Juan stepped on stage and began his service, which was surprisingly well done. Nothing against Juan, but I actually had fun listening to him. He talked about his prison life, his homeless life, and what he'd been doing since. I marveled that a church would let a man like him up on the podium—and for a brief moment, I had some actual respect for them. *Some of them.*

There were some of them who walked up, shook my hand, and spat out the same jargon you'd hear during a Pizza Corp conference call. People who talked about helping the poor but whispered that immigrants should go back to their native countries under their breath.

But there were some, the shy ones, who I could tell really believed what they were saying. A couple walked up to us and asked if we'd seen the latest super hero movie… it caught me off guard in the best of ways. They invited us over to a party that they were planning on hosting in a few weeks.

They didn't even know us… but they invited us to their house. To do something that wasn't inherently religious, no less.

Trinity wanted to go.

We told them we'd go.

It felt nice—the potential of having friends.   Having something to look forward to, like a party.

After the service was finished, that was all we could think about. We went back home, sat on the bed—we didn't lay down, we sat on the covers, like teenagers—turned on old Star Wars movies and talked again for hours about what the next movie would be like, if they were going to stop making them, and that both of us were glad that we got to share whatever new movies came out together.

Then we talked about other things… things we talked about in the car before, then things that we hadn't.

And then—we did something that we hadn't had time or energy to do in nine months…

We kissed.

And then, we kissed some more.

Before we knew it, we were under the covers, discovering each other's bodies for what felt like the first time.

I was nervous, if you can believe it.

This was the woman I'd spent *years* sleeping next to. I spent half of a decade seeing her face every single day—when I got home from work, when we went to bed, and when I woke up… and I was *nervous.*

That night, I held her tighter than I'd ever held a person. I wanted every inch of her touching me. I didn't want her to be taken away from me... and I'd be damned if I'd let the world try.

She rested in my arms for the rest of the night.

After she fell asleep, the realities of the world started to surface again... but I knew that, starting the day after tomorrow, I was free to spend forever with her...

After making it to work early the next morning, I first and foremost made sure to tidy everything up—there was still a pile of dishes in the sink, trash in the lobby garbage cans, as well as a ton of other small stuff that was left over from the day before. It wasn't on my behalf—if Kyle asked why the place was a mess, I could always just pin it on Crabby, but I didn't want to. Sunday nights are always chaotic and we were always short handed. Crabby might be frustrating at times, but it wasn't her fault.

Juan came in while I was in the middle of tidying up—we made some small talk but I didn't feel like taking it beyond, "I liked your sermon last night," and "Yeah, Trinity's due date's tomorrow."

I just couldn't shake the rest of my thoughts away.

Up until this point, at every doctor's appointment that I was able to attend, they made sure to remind us countless times of the risk for miscarriage or postpartum hemorrhaging. In other words, Trinity and the baby were in danger... and there was a tremendous risk for us to come home leaving one of them behind. *And it was impossible to know which one.*

My dismissiveness was inescapable—when it came up in conversation, it wasn't like I *wanted* to ignore Trinity, her family, or the situation... but my anxiety about the future of the two people I loved most was drowning me. If I started one thought, it would inevitably lead to an avalanche—so I remained distant. Uninvolved. *Objectively unresponsive* about the whole ordeal. So much so that I could tell that my silence was slowly killing her. I was potentially more toxic than the cancer itself.

Kyle unlocked the lobby door and sat himself down at table one just minutes before the store opened. He said nothing until his laptop and paperwork were all laid out in front of him. Once everything was a go, he made his way behind the counter and exchanged his usual acknowledgements with me about our store's *wins* and *opportunities.*

I, in exchange, plastered on a fake smile and a synthetic customer oriented attitude. After a brief jabber, Kyle sat back down at the table and typed pseudo-engagingly into his laptop.

After an hour or so, George walked in for his first day of work. I thought Kyle would have something to say about it, but even when he looked up toward us, George's face didn't register to him. It was a relief.

I walked George through setting up his username, which he was quick to admit that I didn't have to do since he'd lost his username and password several times before—and by this point he had Crabby's credentials memorized, so he just typed hers in to give himself authorization to change his.

"BossMan," he said, "I've probably done this more times than you have."

And then he proceeded to finish, without my help.

When he was all settled in, I went back and grabbed a name-badge from the bucket, printed a sticker onto it, and walked over to him.

"This is coming from Janice... as much as I'd like to take credit for it," I told him, "but we're hiring you back on one condition and one condition alone."

And then I gave him his new name-badge, which had his proper name, *Luca Martinez*, printed on it.

In my entire time knowing George, there had only been three times he was speechless... and this was the first time.

We continued to make the few orders that came in at open that morning and it took another thirty minutes or so before Kyle made his way behind the counter once again and asked for me to join him. I made sure George and Juan had things handled and I walked into the lobby and sat down.

The entire meeting was wrapped up in a matter of minutes—and to be honest, as hyped up for it as I should have been, it ended up feeling hollow, and I can't express why.

At first, we began by going over my goals listed in my PDP, then we went over my strengths—*which was a conversation that turned out to be surprisingly lengthy*, followed by my opportunities—*which ended up being surprisingly short.* Subsequently, we talked over the same about my store, then the district, then the area. All of this was typical and predicted.

And then... he did something that surprised me.

He offered me the job.

"Just like that?"

"Just like that."

I'd start training when I returned from my leave, which would be a full two weeks. No rescheduling, no sudden changes, *no ifs, ands, or buts.*

"A position opened up at the Manchester St. location," he said.

It was everything I wanted—with only one complication: I'd have to come into work the following day.

"It's only a half-day," he said, "you'd be out by noon at latest. Your wife is induced at what time?"

"Eleven-thirty."

"You'll have time to get there before the baby's born. Labor takes several hours. She probably won't be but a few centimeters by then."

Kyle knew about Trinity's situation. He knew everything there was to know—but because he was the only district manager to give me the time of day, I felt a sense of trust toward him that I'd never felt before with anyone above me... except for Janice.

And, like an idiot, I accepted.

When the meeting was over, Kyle gathered his things and left after a quick *meet and greet* with Juan and George. Handshakes ensued without much else. The rest of the shift went by semi-smoothly. We had the occasional rush, but with George as an extra person on the schedule it was pretty stress-free... other than my feeling as conflicted as ever.

I had a lot of mixed emotions—I was excited that I was finally getting what I wanted, I was scared that just tomorrow morning I'd potentially miss a part of the birth of my baby, I was anxious about how to tell Trinity... but most of all, I felt empty.

This wasn't how I thought this climb would end. I had reached the top of the mountain after months of excursion, only to find that it was half the height that it had seemed while I stood looking at it. The view at the top was abysmal—other mountains completely obstructing everything I wanted to see. After the massive ascent to which *I had given my everything*, all that was in front of me was the way back down... and all it would've taken was a small push to be back where I started.

I felt the deep sinking feeling that none of it was worth it.

After the shift, I found myself back at the retail store and I couldn't for the life of me find anything that could make the situation better. I wanted to give Trinity something. I wanted to show her that I loved her... but nothing on the shelves could do that.

I spent hours in the store... and I wished I could spend it with Trinity, but truth be told I was biding my time. I was stalling. I didn't want to tell her what happened... and I didn't want *tomorrow to come*, but more than anything else *I wanted it gone.*

Eventually, I found that recognizable symbol. It was printed on the front of a spiral notebook. It was perfect. I knew that it wouldn't make any of this up to Trinity, but after thirty more minutes of searching I cut my losses and purchased it. An hour later, I made it home with the notebook... and the news.

Trinity's disappointment in me was palpable. So was her

anxiety about the next day. And so was my feeling that she never deserved me...

She asked me to call out.

I told her that I had already told Kyle that I would come in.

She told me to leave early tomorrow.

I told her I'd try.

We went to bed early that night. Neither of us said another word to each other—and neither of us slept.

CHAPTER 9

I was done, *at least that's what I told myself,* with all of the bullshit. I got my promotion, George was re-hired, Max was promoted, and I was all set up to take my leave of absence. All that I had left was one more day. One more *short* day. I was off at twelve. Five more hours... And then... it was finally time for *me*. *My* family. *My* life.

My arm froze as I reached my hand out to hit the snooze button on my phone alarm. I snapped it back under the covers and felt Trinity's warmth against my skin as I listened to the solemn sound of the rain. I couldn't believe that I got suckered into working another day at Pizza Corp before my leave. Especially not today. I tried to pull the sheets over my head, shielding myself from the freezing air by the window but before I could, they were yanked from me.

"Tony," said Trinity, "get up."

It was seven in the morning. I had work at eight and I had promised I'd walk Trinity to her car. She hadn't much talked to me. I couldn't blame her. I tried telling Trinity that I didn't like it any more than she did... She believed me about as much as you'd expect her to. *Not at all.*

We got dressed without as much as a single word to each other. I got all of Trinity's bags and tried to keep them dry while I loaded them into the car. I loaded the baby's stuff, most of it under my shirt to protect them, then grabbed Trinity's purse and carried it out for her... I walked her out, holding an umbrella over her head and opening the door for her. I tried to kiss her as she sat down... but she turned away.

Yeah.

Yeah...

"I, um..." I said.

I handed her the umbrella and she shut the door.

The chilling rain drenched my hair like a flooding river

against a grassy plain. The pellets of rain drops battered against my uniform as I hung my head, turned back around, and whispered to myself, so quietly that I wasn't sure anything actually came out of my mouth.

"I love you," I said and heard the car drive off into the distance.

Pulling up at Pizza Corp, I turned the frosty steering wheel into the empty parking space. In my rear-view mirror was George, soaking wet and sitting on the curb like a stray puppy. I walked up to the door, unlocked it, and let him in.

"Dude. What are you doing here?" he asked.

I... really had to think about the answer.

"I'm, um, working," I said.

"Oh," he said and left it at that, marking the second time in his life that he was completely speechless.

We walked in and listened to the nothingness that was the unoccupied Pizza Corp building. The patters of rain calmed my nerves a bit, although I couldn't stop thinking about everything I'd done and everything I had promised I would do. I flipped the light-switch and let the kitchen lights take their sweet time before turning on. It was calming, in a way. There was something peaceful and familiar about it. I didn't want to be there... but being there made me feel better about it. I don't know. It's hard to explain.

"Good morning, Pizza Corp," said George as he popped open a bag of gummy worms, shook his hair dry, and grabbed the dough out of the fridge.

I took a large, deep breath.

"*Good morning, Pizza Corp,*" I sighed.

Four more hours...

"Thanks for calling Pizza Corp," I said, "This is Tony, will this be delivery or carryout?"

"Hey Tony, it's Janice," she said.

Finally, a friendly voice.

I logged into the computer to print out the schedule and daily paperwork. It made a loud noise and promptly decided not to. A few kicks and sporadic button presses later it did what I asked but wasn't happy about any of it. I looked at the clock on the wall. Nine a.m.

"I was just checking in on you," Janice said. "Kyle told me that your wife is being induced today."

"Yep..." I told her. "I'm okay."

"You sure?" she asked.

"Yeah…" I said.

She sighed.

There was a bit of a silence. Neither of us was sure what to say at that point. After that day, she'd no longer be my boss. We'd gotten pretty close over the last few months. It felt strange that it was going to end while she was out of town. There was also a thick layer of discontent between us. When she was sent out, there was nobody to shield me from being overused and overworked. This was nothing new to me… but I could tell she wished that things were different. She was always a good boss. She protected Crabby and me. She took care of us. I started to wonder about who my next boss would be. Would it be like Janice or Katty, or would it be someone completely different?

"Tony," she said, "when the closer gets there, I want you to leave. I don't care how busy it is. You deserve to be with your family."

"Yeah," I said, "you got it."

"Good. Also… I just wanted to let you know… I'm proud of you. You've gone through a lot since we've started working together… and I'm glad you're finally moving up."

"Thank you," I said, unsure of what else to add.

"Also…" she said, "if Kyle… or anyone else for that matter… asks you to come in during your leave… tell them *very kindly* to fuck off."

I chuckled.

"I'll do that," I told her.

"If you don't," she said, "I'll do it for you. If I was still at the store, I would've been working your shifts all week. You know that. You don't have to be there... *I know why you are...* and I appreciate it, but—"

She paused, took a breath, and then in a calm, managerial, motherly voice continued.

"Just..." she said, "let me know if you need me."

I could tell she was repressing other things. *Guilt* probably being the most predominant. She'd been telling me all month that she'd call Kyle and convince him to schedule my leave for me, but I refused. I wanted this promotion. I wanted to be, *as much as I hated to say it,* where I was. This wasn't her fault. Although... in just three hours I will have wished it was... *but I had no one to blame but myself.*

I put the clipboard on the counter. The schedule, paperwork, everything—it was all ready for the next manager to take over. I walked around toward the hallway and flipped on the lobby lights. One group at a time, each flickered rapidly until they were fully lit. I'd seen it a million times but for some reason I took note this specific time. There was nothing different about it, other than the fact that I was leaving soon, but it felt special in a way. This was the last time I'd be opening at this store. I guess I didn't fully process it until then. I was leaving... this was my last day here. Soon, I'd be at some new store, getting to know some new crew, processing some different paperwork... turning on different lights.

After a few moments of staring aimlessly at it, I felt a pat on my shoulder.

"Hey man," said Reece, "congrats."

I turned back to him, faked a smile, and immediately knew what he was going to say next. Placing the guitar strap behind his neck, he played a few notes and warmed up his delicate but *deep* voice. He raised his eyebrow and gave me a grin.

"Just one song," he said, "come on. It's a day of celebration."

"Max isn't here," I said.

"Max is at another store," he said without a second's hesitation, almost like he knew the trajectory of my thoughts and was lining up the shot.

I thought about arguing with him but realized that I had no idea why. It *was* a day of celebration. George was back. I was promoted. My baby was being born. In just two hours, I was going to start a new life. Today was, in every possible aspect, a day worth celebrating.

I sighed and pulled the most optimistic thought from a deep corner of my mind. I looked through the kitchen and got a set of measuring spoons that had a history of beating on the make-table like a drum set while we played. George grabbed a gigantic funnel and used it as a brass instrument, and we ceremoniously scolded him and promised to never use that funnel again, then counted down the music.

The chorus, as I have previously mentioned, goes like this:

It's thirteen,

Thirteen fifty-three,

After taxes and delivery,

That two-fifty doesn't go to me,

But hey,

That's the price that you paid,

It's thirteen fifty-three,

I'd say it sounded fantastic... but I'd be lying my ass off. It sounded like us, though. It sounded like it always used to... and in that moment it made me feel, for the very last time, at home.

And here we go again...

Pizzas flew out of the oven like turds from a swarm of seagulls. Trying to sort them, I placed the pizzas belonging to the same order off in separate stacks. The second that I made a small dent at the cut-table, the ear-splitting siren from the fryer cried desperately for someone to take care of the wings that were about to burn in the grease. I kept my cool. As selfish as it was to say, it didn't matter. It was eleven thirty... I was almost there. Half an hour more.

"Where's number one-forty-one?!" I shouted.

"I don't know!" said George. "Didn't you already box it up?!"

My phone vibrated continuously in my pocket. I told myself I'd check it when the next guy came in to relieve me. I'd just toss him the clipboard, clock out, and check my phone on my way to the car. It didn't matter. It was only thirty minutes away. Whoever it was could wait.

I slipped as I raced toward the wings, catching myself on the sauce-table. Adjusting my footing on the slick, greasy floor, I looked at the screen showing the orders. There were so freaking many. An order for sixteen boneless, fourteen traditional, and eight breaded traditional to start. Plus numerous tickets laying around on the table, no doubt from someone trying to save our store's performance scores.

Looking in the grease, most of them were nearly black. Eh, whatever. Close enough.

"Does it have wings?!" I asked.

George stopped and clicked a few buttons on the make-table computer, making beeps and buzzes at every press.

"No!" said George and pressed a few more buttons, "wait— yeah!"

"Which one?" I asked.

"Order one-forty-one!" he said.

Ugh.

"Wings or no?!" I asked.

"Uh," he said, "yes on the wing fryer. No on the wings. They ordered cheese sticks."

"Oh." I said, "That makes sense."

Someone rang the stupid "Ring for Service" bell. After half a second, they rang it again. This time, they blared it like an alarm, one ring after another, non-stop until they heard a response.

"I'll be right with you!" I shouted across the kitchen.

The bell continued to ring.

"One second!" I yelled.

The ringing stopped… momentarily. I got the cheese sticks set aside and put them into the delivery bag. Walking slowly, trying to be careful not to accidentally answer my damn phone, I made my way to the counter.

"How can I help you?" I asked.

"Number One-Forty-Five!" she said.

She glared at me and slammed the receipt on the table.

"You said fifteen minutes!" she said. "Look at the time on the ticket!"

The driver-door chimed and burgled my attention from her, although I never took my eyes from hers. I hoped that it could be the next manager. I didn't know his name, appearance, or anything about him. I had no idea what *or who* to look for… but maybe, just maybe that was him. Maybe in just a few seconds, I'd turn around and see him clocking in, then I could go.

"I'm sorry ma'am—" I started.

"—Look at the ticket!" she shouted.

I looked at it.

"It says you ordered it at eleven twenty-nine," I said.

I looked at the clock.

"It's eleven forty three." I said. "I'm sorry about the wait, ma'am, it will be just a few—"

I realized that I still had fifteen minutes. It was doubtful that whoever this guy was would get here this quickly. I couldn't get my hopes up. It wasn't him, I thought. *It wasn't him.*

"—My watch says eleven forty-seven!" she said.

"I'm sorry, ma'am—" I started.

But maybe it *was* him. *Maybe this was my last customer at this store. Maybe after this confrontation, I could leave and be with my family. Maybe this was it. Maybe, just maybe—*

"Look at my watch!" she said.

I looked at her watch.

It was white gold, with a thick, circular face that read eleven forty-seven.

"Yes ma'am," I told her and waited for her to respond.

She didn't.

"It will be a few minutes," I said, "our clocks are a little behind yours. I'm sorry about the wait. We're running a little behind today, we've been really busy."

I turned around for just a second, finding no one. *Who had walked in?* I took another glance, looked toward the wing-station, the cut-table, the make-table, everywhere... There wasn't anyone—

"And that's *my problem?!*" the customer shouted.

The line behind her started to build up as a small crowd of people walked through the door. The driver door chimed once more. I quickly turned toward it and saw nothing amiss except for a missing delivery bag—it was a driver.

"Ma'am, I apologize," I said. "It will be a few minutes."
I called for the next customer, looked toward the rest of the line, and felt my phone vibrate once again in my pocket. *Fifteen more minutes,* I told myself, *just fifteen more damn minutes.* I continued onto the next customer, then the next—and twenty minutes later, the driver door chimed once again…

Okay, where is this guy?!

I was supposed to be off an hour ago! We'd been non-stop, I hadn't had the chance to take a piss let alone check my damn phone. It shouldn't have been this busy—it was a Monday. What was going on today? Was there a special promotion going on that I didn't know about?

"My order's ready!" shouted the customer. "That screen says it's ready!"

Yes. You're right. Take a fucking chill pill. I'll get there in a second.

I tossed the wings, shoved them into the box, and threw it into the delivery bag on top of the stack of about fifty.

"Where are the drivers?!" I asked.

"Reece was just here!" said George. "I think he took three of them. I haven't seen anyone else."

I looked at the clock. One fifteen. *What the hell.* I needed to call Kyle and ask him where the hell whoever the hell was, but I didn't have the time—the customers were like scavengers picking meat from bones, preying on every last millisecond I had.

And then... in the blink of an eye, everything took a turn for the worst.

Like shards of shattered glass, a familiar sound pierced through my ears from the parking lot. George and I paused for a moment, together—hoping that we were wrong. The shrieking sound of school bus breaks echoed through the lobby... Running up toward the counter to peek through the windows, we knew in an instant that everything during this shift had changed... and we were inarguably, unquestionably, undeniably, and indisputably *absolutely fucked.*

"Oh," said George, which was the third and last time in his entire life that he'd been in a loss for words.

The lobby doors opened and a flood of children ran inside—yelling, screaming, and throwing things everywhere.

We weren't, would never be, and couldn't have possibly been prepared for a school bus. And there we were. The lobby line was filled throughout with kids looking at menus, hitting each other with them, and throwing them on the floor.

And, soon, fifty seven orders of personal pan pizzas showed

up on our screen.

They were out. The lobby was messy, the store was a wreck, and there were still a ton of delivery orders on the make-table screen, but we got the kids out. Whenever the closing manager got there, the trade-off would be easy. The shift would suck, but at least I'd be able to hand him the clipboard. I took a moment and realized that I had a few seconds to spare, so I reached my hand into my pocket to grab my phone. The first thing I did was look at the time—Three o'clock.

And of course, the store phone rang again.

"Thank you for calling Pizza Corp," I said. "This is Tony. Will this be delivery or carryout?"

"Hey Tony," he said, "it's Kyle."

Fifty-three text messages, thirty-nine missed calls, and twenty eight voicemails.

All from Trinity's phone.

"Hey, bud, I know you were supposed to be off already. John from Beach Street just called out," he said. "I've been working hard to get someone in to replace you. You'll be out of there in a few hours. If all else fails, Crabby comes in at five. She'll relieve you then."

I was *stunned.*

Unlocking the phone, I was hit with the first several of Trinity's messages...

"Tony... Please come up here," one said.

"I'm sorry, okay?! I need you..." said another.

"Have you..." I told Kyle, *"have you tried calling Crabby?"*

The stupid bell rang, meaning another customer arrived at the counter. The bell rang again, then again.

"Hello?" A raspy voice said from the counter.

"Well, not quite yet," he said. "She's scheduled her full forty hours for the week. We don't want her going into overtime."

"Tony, this is Trinity's mother. There's been a complication. We need you in the delivery room," another said.

"Overtime," I said.

"Tony, where are you?!" said another one.

"Exactly," Kyle said. "Don't worry, bud. You'll be out of there in no time."

"Really?!" the customer shouted. "I need to pick up an order! I'm in a hurry!"

"I know we need your promotion... Can we start over somewhere else? Can you just quit and be with me? I promise we'll be okay. I need you," said another text.

I scrolled to the bottom of the list and noticed something that caught me completely off guard... The last message was from one forty-five—over an hour ago. I hadn't received anything since an hour ago other than a voicemail from a number that I didn't recognize.

The bell rang again, this time continuously.

"Just hang in there," said Kyle, "we'll get you somebody."

"Come on!" said the customer.

Everything stood still, silent, and dead as I flipped through my phone and read my last visual voicemail message... a message that I'll never forget, never fully process, and never unsee.

It was from the hospital.

"Okay," I told Kyle, and hung up.

What had I done?

Walking passed George at the cut-table, I heard the dishes clank together but couldn't recognize them. The "Ring for Service" bell chimed, non-stop, in my mind's rearview mirror. The tight space in the kitchen seemed ever-reaching. Taking each step took an eternity.

This was my fault. I could've been with her. During her final thoughts, her final breaths, I was the one she reached out to... and I was gone. I left her.

We had spent years painting a canvas that was instantly washed clean, as if nothing had ever been on it. The laughter, the sorrow, the pain, and the pleasure were completely dried in the blink of an eye and reduced to numbness, and nothingness... and I wasn't even there to witness it. It was as if she had never existed, and the world had forgotten how to describe her. The universe itself paused in her absence, but was forced to continue aimlessly onward without her.

I couldn't help but wonder what her last thought was. Was she waiting for me, honestly believing that I'd be there with her? Or had she given up on me?

Every moment stretched for a thousand miles. After each instant, I felt imprisoned by the dawning realization that I'd have to reach the next second of my life.

Walking out into the kitchen, opening the door of the future that never should've been, I was blinded by the light of my reality- - a fantasy that was only prevalent in the darkest corners of my mind... A monstrous realization would haunt me until my last breath. The universe around me was made of three undeniable truths: Trinity was gone. I was alone. I wanted to die.

And yes, more than anything in the whole world, I wanted to die.

"What the hell?!" the customer shouted. "Do you know how long I've been waiting?!"

I could see Trinity waiting in the bed, wondering where I was... as she screamed helplessly and directionless in the worst pain she'd ever been in...

In the stretch of forever that was the next few moments, I told myself I'd throw everything away and let that customer have it. There'd be nothing I wouldn't say. I'd yell, cry, and tell her that she can *fucking wait a minute...* nothing I could say would be perfect, but I was sure I would let her know everything that I was thinking...

... But I opened my mouth and said, "I'm sorry ma'am. *Thank you for your patience.* I'm happy you came in today. If you'll give me a quick minute, I'll be right with you." Like a good little robot.

Yeah.

The fact that I couldn't stand my ground for anyone highlighted in my darkest hour who I truly was. I was a flimsy, soulless and robotic *shadow of a person.*

And then it dawned on me... smashing me like a van through a glass wall—I'd never see her again. I'd never get to kiss her, or talk to her, or run my fingers through her hair, or wrap my arms around her... or apologize to her—ever. Not another single time.

So then I walked to the back, grabbed the largest, sharpest knife I could find and snuck into the restroom, locking the door behind me.

I rested it on my wrist... the blade stretched down my forearm. All it would've taken was just a little pressure and I'd be gone. Nothing could stop me. No one could call me in for another day. No one could tell me *"hang on, just one more thing,"* it'd be over. That'd be it. For once and for all.

I'd been thinking about this for a long while, you know. This wasn't just some overdramatic reaction. I'd been waiting for this... patiently—*for the last six months*—with only one thought stopping me. If I had killed myself before that day, she would have had to go it alone... and I couldn't do that to her—*but what did it matter now?!*

Soon, *I thought,* it would end anyway. Soon, I'd be with Trinity. I'd have my family. I'd not only get to end this life, but I'd start a new one *with her.*

I never told anyone, *not even you,* but don't think for a second that it wasn't on the forefront of my mind. *Would you have tried to save me if you had known me?* Would you, knowing the deepest, *darkest* of my thoughts, have walked over to me and asked me *if I was feeling okay?* Why not? Because it would've been *awkward?* Because you might have been *wrong?* Maybe I *was* fine? *Maybe I was just having a bad day? Maybe it wasn't your problem?*

Well there I was. With a knife against my wrist. And there was nothing you could've done about it now—there was nothing you could take back anymore—there were no last words you could've said.

In just a few minutes, they'd find me. They'd break open the bathroom door after seeing the blood flood out into the lobby. And they'd see me, laying there, motionless, breathless, lifeless—and they'd *have to pay attention.* They'd have to call the ambulance. They'd have to tell the police. They'd have to tell corporate... and they wouldn't have time for anything else. Customers would line up at the counter, orders would come in online, and they'd bitch and complain that they weren't getting service... because for the first time in their miserable lives, *they wouldn't matter.* They'd wait and watch while the food trapped itself at the end of the oven... and they would just have to deal with it. All of my friends and partners would mourn for me, unsure of what to do or who to call or if I'd survive—*while the customers stared at the empty, silent kitchen, watching the nothingness, waiting for someone to help them...*

But I waited too long...

The doorknob shook, slowly at first, then violently. It stopped for a half second and then, immediately, unexpectedly, and *loudly* turned a full circle. *Someone had a key.*

I stared at the door, clueless about what to do next. *Who was coming in? If it was the temporary manager, this would be the only thing they'd ever know about me. Was it George? Was it Kyle?! Who else has a key and would know about the situation?! I looked at the blade—and my arm—and realized that I needed to make this quick. I needed to finish this right now...*

But before I could think twice about it, the door flew open and nearly hit me in the face. Her worried face flashed to anger— and the terrifying sight of her bulgy body running toward me was more horrifying than death... *or life.*

This, *once again,* is what Crabby looked like:

I wanted to run, but I couldn't move my legs... I couldn't stand up—I couldn't look away. From completely stationary to rocketing toward me like a torpedo, it seemed like the universe launched her toward me... and I couldn't escape.

Without a single word, she grabbed the top of the blade and flung it away. She took a second, but only a second, to think about how to approach me... and before I could blink, she grabbed the neck-line of my shirt and threw me against the wall so hard I was worried I crushed it under my skull.

"What the hell?!" she growled, and just held me there until I responded.

She put just enough weight into my collar bone to hold me up. After a moment, I started slipping down my shirt, but with a forceful push she had me right back up on the wall where she wanted me.

"Tony!" she barked. *"What. The. Hell."*

"I can't—" I told her, but couldn't breath—and not because of her. Her fist trapped my lungs, but my thoughts trapped my words.

"You can't—" she roared, *"You can't what?!* You can't live anymore?! No one can love you anymore?! You can't love anyone else?! *What can't you do?!"*

She pulled her snarling, infuriated face toward me. Her eyes beamed into mine, forcing me to remember pieces of myself that I wanted to forget.

"I can't..." I whispered, "I can't tell her I love her. I'll never be able to apologize. I'll never have another chance."

She eased her grip and I felt the blood rush back into my chest as she put me down. Her eyes widened, not losing focus from mine.

In an instant, she knew. Just looking into my eyes, she connected the dots. She knew everything.

"No..." she said, "you may not be able to."

Slowly, she moved her hands from my shirt and placed one behind my back, giving me a gentle, loving rub. She ran the fingers from her other hand through the hair on the back of my head as she pulled me into her chest.

"She knew, though," Crabby said. "She knew all of those things. You didn't *have* to tell her."

Crabby sat me down at table one and walked toward the doors and locked them. Coming by to check on me, she asked for my phone... I gave it to her without thinking... then she made her way toward the kitchen. A few moments later I heard her tell something to George and then she walked back toward me.

"What are you doing?" I asked her.

The chair squealed as she sat down across from me.

"I'm closing the lobby. George is calling helpdesk to turn the online carryout orders off," she said.

"What about corporate?" I asked. "You could get fired."

"Yeah," she said, "and they can fuck themselves."

"Why?" I asked.

"Because that voicemail says that you still have someone waiting on you and I'm driving you up there. There's no way I'm going to let you go alone."

Hold on—Time shook the earth and shattered reality once again.

I forced myself to say the words, "... Who? Who's waiting for me?"

She pulled the keys from her purse and unlocked the door to her car—her blinkers shined through the lobby windows.

"She doesn't have a name yet," she said.

"Who?!" I said again.

She sighed, got up, and walked around the table to grab my hand.

"Your daughter," she said. "Come on."

"Daughter?" I asked.

It was a girl?

287

The smell of hand sanitizer burned my nostrils as the doors slid open. Several nurses sat at a counter, each helping someone—everyone stressed out, sick, or crying. About fifty people sat in the lobby. I recognized some of them... Trinity's family. They all looked either worried, exhausted, or just... staring into the infinity and uncertainty that was the seat in front of them. There was no closure... they were all in intermittent purgatory, waiting for information that they all hoped they'd never receive.

Crabby talked to everyone for me. I didn't have to stop and ask where to go, or what I should do. Crabby took care of everything... I just had to follow her. The hospital was an infinite maze of hallways and doors. Walking by, I overheard a nurse ask a patient at check-in if he had any thoughts of suicide—his answer, *"Not recently,"* gave him a pass. The nurse thanked him, laughed, and said, *"It's a lot of paperwork."*

I couldn't help but wonder how recently "*not recently*"was. If they had asked me that day, I would've said something similar. It's not exactly something you'd tell strangers. In a strange way, I was relieved that "*not recently*" didn't draw any red flags—I stored that response in the back of my mind in case I ever needed it.

The last doorway slammed open and we snuck through... and I knew we had arrived where we were trying to go. I never realized until that point that babies had a particular smell—and during what little thought I put into it, I thought it would smell like poop and vomit. But that wasn't it at all. It smelled... *smooth*... and soft. It *smelled* how laying down after relaxing day *felt.* I couldn't explain it. It smelled like... nostalgia.

A nurse guided us toward a glass window... and that was when I first saw her.

I wish I could say I knew which one she was right away, or even that I was able to find her by myself... but I'd be lying if I did. The nurse pointed her out to me, in the middle of the room... surrounded by countless others. She was sleeping peacefully, silently, and completely still—completely unaware of what had happened in her life just a few hours before. Completely unaware that the woman who gave birth to her was taken from her... For the first time that day, there was some relief. There was someone, *someone who I loved very, very much*... who was happy.

"Would you like to hold her?" the nurse asked.

I didn't want to wake her up... I've seen sitcoms. I know how waking up a baby goes.

"No, thank you." I said, "... but may I sit next to her?"

I sat and watched her sleep for hours. Crabby never left my side, except for a few moments when she went for some coffee.

I couldn't believe that I was a father... I had a daughter... and there she was right in front of me. Who could have known that after such horrifying events brought her here, she was able to rest so peacefully? It was mesmerizing how relaxed she was. Every few minutes or so, she'd stop moving completely and I'd nearly panic until I saw her chest lift up with a full breath of air. She had Trinity's nose... and her brown hair. In a way, she gave me the closure I needed... Trinity was gone, but the baby would forever be here in her place.

I almost resented her.

If this baby had never existed, Trinity would have still been with me and our lives would have been completely different. I still would have been at the firm, she would've still been working, we would have still had our own place... and we would've had the chance to fight the cancer that killed her.

But it wasn't the baby's fault. It was mine.

After a few hours, a nurse came by with some food from the cafeteria. I refused at first... I couldn't afford it, but she insisted and told me that she'd already paid for it.

"You're the father, right?" she asked.

I was ashamed. What kind of *father* would let his wife die alone? No, I was not a *father*. I was a man of no importance. I had caused this... and I had let everyone who I hurt and killed die *alone*.

Don't call me a father.

She handed me the plate of Salisbury steak, mashed potatoes, and green beans and put her backpack on the ground next to her.

I nodded and promptly ignored the food, concentrating again on the baby. While the nurse ruffled through her bag, the smell of the steak started to tempt me and eventually I took a bite.

"She left something for you," said the nurse.

I turned to her as she pulled out the spiral notebook... the one I had just gotten Trinity.

"She was writing in it this morning," the nurse said. "She told me what she was writing about... the best feelings in the world... and I asked her to read some of them to me."

I put the plate on the floor and she handed it to me. It smelled like Trinity's hair... and I let a few tears slip from my eyes when I realized that I'd never smell it again.

"I could tell she loved you," she said.

"How?" I asked.

"Just read them," she said.

I opened it... and read through it. She wrote down the

ones that we had made together… and added a few.

The new list looked like this:

	The Best Feelings in the World
12.	Staying up late watching a movie you love
13.	Meeting new friends—the kind of friends you know will last forever…
14.	The look in Tony's eyes when he says he loves me.
15.	Sitting on the bed and just talking… for as long as I want.
16.	Pretending I am asleep so I can feel him hold me… knowing he never wants to let go.
17.	Hearing him wake up and whisper to himself his most secret thoughts… and knowing some of them are about me.

"Thank you," I told her.

"You're welcome," she said.

"Did you two talk about what you were going to name her?" she asked.

I shook my head no.

"We didn't even know the gender," I said.

She nodded and sighed.

"I do know what name I'd like, though," I said.

"What's that?" she asked.

"Trinity's middle name," I said. "Rachel."

After a few more minutes, Crabby told me that she needed to head back to close the store. I didn't realize until then how much time had passed... but it was eleven. Pizza Corp was closed. Poor George had been there all night by himself.

The nurses understood the situation... *as well as I could expect them to.* They let me leave after I told them I'd be back in a few hours. I didn't have the car seat anyway. I couldn't take her home as it was. But I could help that everyone at the hospital was judging me for being a terrible father... and a horrifyingly bad husband.

We were a few blocks away from Pizza Corp... the time inched on again. I was in such a hurry to get back to Pizza Corp so I could drive back to the hospital and see my baby... But a dreadful thought occurred to me. After I packed up my daughter's things and got in the car... I would have nowhere to go. I'd been living with Trinity's parents. I didn't have a home to go to. I had nothing. All I had was Pizza Corp.

The asphalt crumbled underneath the tires while the car squeaked into the parking space. I took a breath and opened the door...

Standing out in the dark, empty lot, I stared toward Pizza Corp's bright, fluorescent red sign, greeting me the way it always did. It was familiar... warm... *and I hated every inch of it.* The lights were all off. The night was over.

"Hey," said Crabby, getting out of the car.

I turned toward her... but she wasn't talking to me. I looked back toward the shadows next to the driver door to see who the hell she was looking at.

"You got him?" Crabby asked.

"Yeah..." said Max, "I've got him."

Max?

The gentle plops of her footsteps hurried toward me—then there she was, rushing up and without a moment's notice wrapping her arms around me. She smothered her face into my chest and pulled herself closer... until there was no separating us.

"Hey," she whispered through my shirt, "Crabby told me what happened."

She pulled tighter, squeezing herself into me... and for the first time that night, even though it felt like the world was falling apart, everything I knew was wrong, and everything that I'd ever wanted was shattered right in front of me... I felt like maybe, just maybe, I had some sort of significance. She was going to protect me. Nothing else could hurt me. I was finally *safe*.

*I closed my eyes, put the weight of my head on hers, and
cried.*

"It's okay," she whispered, *"It's okay..."*

"I've got you," she said.

We sat on the curb... Crabby and George had left hours
before... Max ran her fingers through my hair as my head rested
in her lap. Every so often she'd throw a rock toward Sonic and
I'd sit up to see how far it would go... then we'd go back to sitting
still. Saying nothing. Just letting the thoughts fly by.

Of all of the endless thoughts and wants and wishes, I
wanted to go back to the hospital and pick up my daughter... but
I didn't even have the car seat with me. I had nothing. Nothing
to use to drive her... and no home to drive to.

I just sat with Max, on the sidewalk, in the silence of the
night... watching the closing crew of Sonic take out the trash.

"Hey Max," I said.

"Yes sir," she said.

I sighed and thought about how to phrase the next few
sentences.

"I just... I just want to say thank you."

"For what?" she said.

There wasn't any other way to say it... so I just said it.

"For responding to Crabby," I said.

She chuckled.

"Anything for you, Tony," she said and continued to rub my head, using what was left of her nails to scratch my scalp.

"So..." I said, "are you and Crabby okay now, I guess?"

She sighed and reached over to grab another rock. I sat up and leaned back on the brick wall, then I realized how much snot and tears I smeared all over her, wondering whether or not I should apologize... I wiped my face on my shirt and tried to make myself comfortable.

"We're getting there," she said and threw a rock.

It landed about halfway to Sonic. I searched my immediate area and scavenged for a rock for myself.

"Can I tell you something?" she asked.

I nodded, barely separating myself from the fog of my thoughts, and tried to peel myself away from them.

She took a breath, slowly, then scurried to find another group of rocks to toss.

"A couple of years ago..." she said, "I had just moved back down here... I had just gotten hired at Pizza Corp, and I was working crazy hours—Dominic got really, really sick. I hadn't finished unpacking, so it was hard to find him warm clothes—it was really hot outside so I didn't think I'd need them—and I didn't have enough money for medicine..."

"And so I just sat with him, while he could barely breathe," she said, "and I thought about how shitty a mother I was, *and how I didn't deserve to have Dominic*, and how I didn't deserve anyone... and how it was all my fault."

She started to let out a tear, but held it in.

"And how if I would've never decided to move away from my husband, Dominic would've been healthy," she said. "So... I tried to kill myself."

I turned toward her, looking deep into her eyes, hoping she'd look back... but she gazed into the stars.

"I told my mom to come and get Dominic... then after everyone was gone, I took about ten sleeping pills... and went to sleep," she said, "and... then I woke up the next day. *And I was so mad...* I didn't want to wake up."

I waited for her to move, speak, or do anything... but for the next few moments, she just sat there with her eyes in the sky.

"And then?" I asked.

"I told my mom," she said, "and I signed up for health insurance through the Obamacare trades... and went to the doctor."

She paused, then rested her eyes into mine.

"And... I got help," she said. "I was always afraid of taking medicine... and *now I'm on it.* You always hear about people being scared of it. You hear all the time about it changing people and forcing people to be happy all the time, and making them not get sad..."

She sighed.

"I still get sad," she said, "I still get worried. Things still build up... and I still get overwhelmed... and it still crushes me."

"What do you mean?" I asked.

She thought about it for a moment... then pulled my head back down in her lap and ran her fingers through my hair again.

"About a week ago, Dominic had his surgery... and it wasn't looking good," she said. "He couldn't even sit up... he just lay there and whimpered... *for an entire day...* And I couldn't stop crying. I was freaking out... I thought I messed everything up again... This was my fault. How could I live with myself if he doesn't make it through this?"

She took a breath... and slowly let it out.

"I kept murmuring, 'he's not going to make it... he's not going to make it... *he's not going to make it.* But in the midst of panicking and crying and hyperventilating and rocking back and forth... what I didn't think was *It's time to kill myself.* Which I *absolutely* would've done before."

"I used to cut myself for less," she said.

"I had chugged liquor until I passed out for less," she said.

"I had considered trying those pills... to put myself to sleep forever... So. Many. Times," she said.

"But I didn't that time. It never even crossed my mind." she said. "I was scared and uncertain and I had no idea what to do... *but I knew I'd still be around to find out.* And Dominic *did* make it... It was a hard night, but *he made it.* And he's better now— *and I'm better now."*

I sat up and pulled my arms around her. To say that we embraced would be an understatement. I held her, and squeezed her, and didn't want to let her go... *And I didn't have to.*

"I'm not leaving you," she said. *"I've got you... for as long as you need me. Just promise me that you'll be here too."*

And so, for the next few hours, I sat in her lap... *and I cried.*

l

CHAPTER 10
THREE YEARS LATER

"Daddy," she said, "Daddy!"

I had drifted off. We'd had a long night last night. I was only out for that few minutes, but every second I could close my eyes counted... and being a single dad with a three year old, tiredness was to be expected.

Opening my eyes and sitting up, taking a moment just to look at my tiny, messy one bedroom apartment, I couldn't stop myself from thinking about how far I had come and what I went through to make sure Rachel had a home, warm food, and someone to take care of her.

It might have been too late, but I had realized that Pizza Corp would never support us—*and no, finding another job was not easy.*

"Daddy! I want to look at pictures!" she shouted.

I sighed.

Rachel pointed at the picture-frame in the hallway. I don't remember when or why I got it—it must have been *years ago.* It was probably a last minute, *"Oh yeah, people usually hang pictures or something"* thing. It was in the shape of a family tree and it held nearly every printed picture we owned. Granted, we didn't have that many.

I picked her up and walked through the maze of birthday balloons. I carefully stepped over Rachel's hastily opened presents and finally we made our way over to the frame. She excitedly shifted herself closer when we moved into the hallway and pushed on my belt with her foot for support.

"Rachel," I said, pulling my pants back up, *"stop..."*

I carried her as quickly as I could and when we got close enough, she calmed down.

We waited for a second so she could tell me what she wanted. Sometimes all she did was look for a second before deciding that she was *bored* and pushed herself away.

"Daddy!" she shouted, *"Who's that?!"*

I looked to see what she was pointing at, but it seemed to be aimless. Her finger's target seemed to change from one second to another.

"Who's who?" I asked.

She huffed.

"Well?" I asked.

She puffed.

Look, kid—I don't know what you want.

Before she blew the house down, I finally got the message. At least, I was pretty sure I did.

"Okay," I said, "who's that?"

I pointed my finger at a picture of Reece at one of his concerts. He never made any money from it, but he always enjoyed volunteering for charity festivals and that sort of thing. In the photo, he played guitar with a few other musicians behind him. *You can guess what song he was playing.*

"Uncle Reece!" she said.

I nodded.

"That's right," I said.

She smiled and sang tunelessly for a moment, then started losing her patience and I was forced to continue.

"Who's that?" I asked.

I pointed to a picture of George—in full Marine uniform. He eventually made it. After he finally got his residency, the Marines took him in and finished off the paperwork for his citizenship. He was officially an American. In the picture, he held Rachel in one hand and his hat in another—he'd just gotten back from Basic Training. In the timeless, perfect moment, they both smiled toward the camera. Rachel held the Batman action figure in front of her and Batman held in front of him a Teamwork Tomato that was taped to his hands.

This is what that Teamwork Tomato looked like:

"—Uncle Luca!" She shouted.

"That's right," I said.

I chuckled for a moment, remembering the first time Rachel called him that.

"Oh! Daddy!—*Daddy!*" she proclaimed, "That's Uncle Luca's Batman!"

She pointed at the Batman action figure on the table.

"That's Uncle Luca! He gave it to me!"

I nodded.

"Yes he did," I said and grinned back to her.

Batman rested on the table, looking quite exhausted himself. He wore a purple dress and a black cape—but not *his* cape, they were a few hand-me-downs kindly given to him by Barbie and Darth Vader. I'm glad they finally sorted their problems out.

Rachel started getting impatient again.

"Who's that?" I asked, pointing to another picture.

She stopped for a moment.

"Oh," she said, "um…"

It made sense… it wasn't a face she got to see every day. In the picture, Trinity and I were sharing our wedding cake. I looked back toward Rachel and the resemblance was uncanny… she looked just like her.

Trinity once asked me what a writer would say about her— how a book would describe her… Well, her warm green eyes were filled with passion—I'll never forget the look on her face when I was in her eyes. It was like I was the center of the universe. Her mind was an ocean of mystery, from the way she thought to the way she acted… to the way she viewed the world. Her personality was captivating—she had me on a string, following her with every step, just waiting for the next moment. She was my everything.

Rachel had her hair, her eyes, her nose... everything. When I looked at her, I could shut my eyes and feel Trinity's arms wrap around me, I could feel her hair brushing my face, and I could hear her soft, gentle voice quietly telling me that there was nothing to worry about... but reality always woke me up and for an instant I felt nothing but silence, darkness and stillness that rested in my mind in her place—but then I'd look back at Rachel and I'd see Trinity's innocent smile... and I knew that she lived on within her. She was still with us.

"That's..." I told her, "that's your Mommy."

"Oh," she said, "Mommy."

"Yeah," I said, and held back a tear, "that's right."

I looked at Rachel for another few seconds and made a relaxed sigh.

"Who's that?" I asked and pointed to a picture of Crabby.

Oh, what the hell. I might as well tell you.

"That's Aunt Olivia!" she said.

I nodded.

Yes, by the way. Olivia was still around. She was still working at Pizza Corp, but she had been a huge help with Rachel. She was *surprisingly* good with kids. It's impressive, trust me.

I looked at a few more pictures of Janice, Juan, and several friends we'd met since... and eventually I decided on one last picture.

"Who's that?" I asked, and pointed to a picture of Max and—

"Dominic!" she shouted.

"That's right," I said. "You know, Dominic's coming over later today... can you go get ready?"

She gasped.

"Dominic's coming over?!" she yelled.

"Yep," I said, "can you go to your room and get some big girl clothes on?"

She ran into her room and started digging through her drawers... and after a few minutes I went in after her to clean everything up and actually find an outfit.

There was a knock at the door and Rachel sprinted toward it.

"Daddy, there's someone at the door!"

I'd told her a million times *not* to do that...

Making my way toward the door, I had to fight with Rachel to get her far enough away to let Max and Dominic in.

"Hey," I said.

She smiled.

"Hey," Max said, "you okay?"

I nodded.

"I just dozed off for a few minutes," I said. "Come on in."

We did this every year—on Rachel's birthday. It was never an easy day for me. Pretty soon she'd be old enough for parties, which I'm sure will make it a little easier, but it's always a struggle to think about where I was three years ago.

"Happy Birthday, Rachel!" said Max, "how old are you?"

Rachel held up a few fingers on each hand and tried to make it out—but she had no idea.

"Two?" she said, holding up four fingers.

Max chuckled.

"You're three now," I told her.

"Three?" she asked.

I leaned down toward her and showed her how to hold up three fingers.

"Hey Rachel," said Dominic, "you want to play with Darth Vader?"

She gasped.

"Darth Vader?!" she said.

Dominic seemed almost grown up. He was six—but he was so calm and gentle for his age. He and Rachel made great friends.

Max and I sat down. Dominic and Rachel ran into her room—Rachel came back half a second later to grab Batman, then sprinted once again to join Dominic.

"Who's paying and who's tipping?" Max asked.

"It's my turn to pay," I said.

"You paid last year," she said.

"Did I?" I asked.

She sighed, got up, and sat down a little closer. I put on a movie and we both sat there silently, just enjoying each other's company.

"I'm paying again," she said. "Did you already order it?"

I nodded.

"You wanted pepperoni, right?" I asked.

"Yep," she said.

"Awesome," I said, "I ordered a large. That should be enough, right?"

We agreed that it should be… and after the movie started we both started to nod off. Drifting away into dreamland, I thought about that last overnight at Pizza Corp that we shared together. I remembered her talking about how she shuffled the cards, but every time she put the Queen of Spades and King of Hearts together on top—and caught myself doing that periodically. I lost my queen, and I'm never getting her back, but I considered Max to be the Queen of Spades to my King of Hearts. It was never a romantic attraction—it was a partnership. No matter how the deck got shuffled, I knew we'd stick together… and no matter what, I knew we'd wind up on top.

We woke up to the doorbell.

… and tiny footsteps.

"Daddy, someone's at the door!"

Dominic caught Rachel in the middle of her sprint down the hall.

"Hold on there, Turbo," he said. "Only grownups can answer the door."

"Grownups?" she asked.

Max and I blinked and rubbed our eyes as the doorbell rang again.

"But they're not getting it," Rachel said.

Slowly, we managed to stand up. I went into the kitchen to find some cash for the tip while Max walked toward the door and answered it.

"See?" said Dominic.

In the living room, while I picked through the jars and grabbed some dollar bills, I overheard their conversation.

"It'll be thirteen fifty-three," he said.

"After taxes?" Max asked, sarcastically.

The driver groaned. That song had been making the rounds.

She handed him a ten and five ones, then took the pizza.

"Hold on one second," she said, "I'll be right back."

She put the pizza on the end table and gave me a shout.

"Did you want cheese and peppers?" she asked.

And then—the driver did something outright surprising.

"Seriously?!" he said, *"I'm fucking done!"*

It didn't occur to us that giving the guy the money and tip separately could insinuate that we wouldn't tip him at all—we were being customers. We did *intend to tip*, but in his mind *right then*, we were the exact people we always hated.

… Although, it took us a few seconds to realize what was happening.

Max raised an eyebrow and walked back toward the door.

"I hate you people!" he shouted. "You piece of shit entitled assholes! *I have kids!* I need tips to survive!"

Just then, Rachel and Dominic raced through the living room and after a small second I walked behind Max… with a ten dollar bill in my hand.

Exasperated, he breathed heavily for a moment until he realized what was happening.

Max and I stood there and looked at him in silence.

Behind us, we overheard Dominic getting Rachel and himself a plate and sit down on the couch, readying themselves to eat. It took Dominic only a few seconds to become completely entranced with the movie.

"Bad day?" I asked.

He sighed.

"I'm sorry," he said.

We laughed it off. We'd been there. In the end, after he left we dug into the pizza—which was beef instead of pepperoni. It was burnt, *somehow cold*, and it took us longer than it should have to realize it was thirty minutes late—but that was to be expected. We had ordered pizza *for delivery*, during the *rush* and during the *ten-dollar special*. We found a way to enjoy it... and we hoped that whoever ended up getting *our* pepperoni pizza found a way to enjoy that too.

And you know what? In the end, we still tipped him.

You know why?

Because we're not *fucking assholes*.

APPENDIUM
A LETTER FROM THE AUTHOR

A while back, I found myself staring at this large kitchen knife. I was slicing tomatoes with it, so I knew how sharp it was... and I wanted to end my life with it, right then and there. My trembling hand still had a loose grip around it; it wouldn't have been that hard to just take it and do it quickly before anyone else realized what happened. It would have been so easy...

I was serious. I was really considering it—no, I was past considering it. My life was getting so hard to live and at that point I was asking myself why I hadn't already ended it. No, you know what? I wasn't asking. I was nagging. I was bitching. That little voice inside of my head was scolding me for my suicide being overdue.

You always hear about suicide as a shocking discovery. The victim's loved ones always come back by saying, "He/she was getting better" or "We just had such a good day, yesterday... he/she was so happy."
Well, in that moment, I figured out a reason for that.

People don't just get "worse" after a good day and decide to end their lives. They end their lives because of the good day. They want their last memories with their loved ones to be perfect. It's a conscious decision. They don't tell the people they love that they're about to commit suicide because the perfection of that last day is perfectly intentional. All they want, literally out of their entire life, is just to live their last few moments worry-free. They don't want to worry about bills, their job, their money, or anything else. They want one good day. Just one. One last memory... and they want it to be perfect. And how do you get that last perfect memory? You plan your suicide right after it's over. That way, you know that you won't have to worry about anything... you can just enjoy the last few moments you have with your family. Suicide is no longer a move of desperation. It's freedom. It's a peace that you feel inside of you, that promises you that you don't have to live with all of these issues anymore. You're done. You can finally sleep.

I convinced myself to put the knife away that day. I still remember how hard it was to hear it slide back into its holster and how impossible it was to remove my hand from it, listening to my boss cuss at me and my co-workers tell me to hurry up. At that point, I was working at a restaurant and was on my sixth twelve-hour shift in a row. It was a hundred and ten degrees inside of the kitchen, we had no air conditioning, sweat was dripping from my forehead into my eyes, I hadn't sat down since four o'clock that morning, and I hadn't eaten anything but a few nibbles in three days. We didn't take breaks, we weren't allowed to. Since I was salaried, I also had to stay as long as business required, without extra pay, which meant two to three hours after my shift was supposed to end every day. And I had to work an extra day every week. Some weeks, I worked all seven days. I couldn't see my friends or my family and I couldn't ask anyone for help. All I could do was get up, go to work, come back home, and go to sleep. By that point, I hadn't seen my two-year-old daughter in weeks. In fact, I remember on occasion hearing her screaming from the other room, begging her mommy to let me stay home from work so I could be with her.

You know that feeling that you get when you drive home after a long day? You zone out, still very much concentrating on driving, but you aren't really there? You turn your brain off so the time goes by faster and you hardly have any energy left to think about anything else anyway? Well, that's how I was feeling—consistently— for two full years. I'd always tell myself that this coming Saturday, or the Sunday the week after, or Monday the next week was going to make it worth it… and then I'd end up working or sleeping right through it. Eventually, I just got to the point where I got so caught up thinking about how I couldn't wait for a later day that I ended up turning my brain off permanently.

One week, I requested a Sunday off so that I could go to an amusement park with my wife and daughter. I had asked for it more than a month in advance. At that point, I was not only contemplating suicide, but planning it. That day was going to be my perfect day, at least, that's what I told myself. However, I knew that if I could make it to that Sunday, I'd be able to convince myself that staying alive was worth it.

But, then, I woke up that morning, got dressed and clocked into work.

I eventually made it through that day, but it took a few more weeks before I finally realized what a mistake I had made in taking that job. I'm grateful for that experience, though. Not only because it taught me some valuable lessons, but because I'm one of the people who survived, and it allowed me to be one of the few to tell these stories. One of the people mentioned in my first dedication did not survive... and I miss her dearly.

It's pertinent that I clarify a few things about the contents of this book. Most everything that has taken place is directly correlated to a real occurrence. However, there are a few things that were stretched and exaggerated.

Firstly, although Pizza Corp is a fictional company, nearly every aspect was taken from other companies that I've worked for. I would like to note, however, that no events, policies, or any other details were taken from my current employer. Not only does the company I work for uphold a set of ideals totally contrary to Pizza Corp's terrible practices, they may have actually saved my life. Their decision to hire me changed my life and the life of my family in ways they'll never fully understand.

Secondly, the incident with Max in Chapter Three was based on three real life scenarios that happened separately. The first one was during a period when I was working for a restaurant and my boss, the store manager, was a single father.

He would bring his daughter up to the restaurant and situations like this one weren't uncommon. It was difficult to keep an eye on her while we were in the middle of a Sunday rush. The second scenario was while I was working at a pizza delivery restaurant—one of my co-workers was chased by a customer. Luckily, she wasn't hurt. The customer ended up denying the whole thing and the store manager ended up sending a male driver to re-deliver the pizza. I disagreed with that decision.

Thirdly, I once worked with a single mom at a retail store. During that time, I was chosen to go through the promotion process, which was very similar to the process described in this book. However, when I chose her as the person to take my spot she was turned down due to her availability and attendance record. She was one of the hardest workers I've ever met. The details in the book regarding external hires and losing them immediately were closely related to real life events.

I would like to point out that some of my most extreme real-life work experiences were left out from the book. Some of my friends and family, while working in the service industry, have been threatened, robbed at gun-point, and were victims of bomb threats. Luckily, everyone that I know made it through those experiences. I myself have been threatened with knives, not only by customers, but by co-workers. Several of my friends, myself included, have had food and products thrown at them during their time in the service industry. One specific occurrence was when a customer threw a fifty-pound weight at one of my cashiers. Luckily, once again, she managed to get out of the way. The wall behind her wasn't so lucky.

I'd like to end this letter by thanking my wonder editor, Laura DuPuy. I've known her nearly my entire life, and she was always there to help me edit, write, rewrite, and re-imagine all of my ideas and scribbles since the very beginning—even the ones that were (and still are) completely unreadable and shall forever be buried in secrecy out of my sheer embarrassment for having written them.

I truly hope you've enjoyed <u>As the Pizza Burns</u> and I hope you'll follow me wherever our next journey takes us. Stay tuned.

Pizza Corp!

Join the family!

Are you looking for a career that can last a lifetime at a company at the cornerstone of its market? Pizza Corp is hiring! We offer paid benefits, flexible scheduling, and excellent promotional opportunities! Find us online with the QR code below!

FLOWCODE

PRIVACY.FLOWCODE.COM